# NOT ME, IT'S A TRAP!

# NOT ME, IT'S A TRAP!

Charles Forest Burton

Illustrated by Mike Ferrin

***Not Me, It's A Trap***

ISBN: 978-1-4951-5370-9



Written by Charles Burton

Illustations by Mike Ferrin mferrin.com



Printed in the United States

Acknowledgements

Thanks to Patricia Rachal for typing and editing my first draft. She laughed at the plot twists, corrected my poor writing skills, and recommended character names that added humor to the story. I am blessed by her desire to have a positive influence on kids and our culture. —Proofnedit@inbox.com

I am grateful to my dear friend, Rebecca Currington of SnapDragonGroup.com, who reviewed, edited, and advised. Her writing skills and knowledge of the publishing industry are valuable resources.

Mike Ferrin's art expresses his true creative gift to transport characters from text to visual images. He drew hundreds of sketches, with few recommendations from me, until I began the final selection process. He is a pleasure to work with and has my sincere appreciation. —www.mferrin.com

Words are inadequate to describe what a gift my wife is to me. She has supported me in every phase and endeavor of my life, including many long days and late nights to help prepare this book for print. She makes me look better than I am, gives me credit when I don't earn it and forgives me when I'm stupid! She is my very best friend.

# Contents

# Plot to Destroy Your Future

## The Discovery

"Hey, Tommy, take a look at this," Dr. Whyze called to his son.

The skinny eleven-year-old hopped up the step stool in front of the counter and stared into a video microscope. After a minute or so, Tommy pulled his head away, rubbed his eyes, and positioned himself for a second look. His freckled face glowed with excitement.

"Wow, Dad!" exclaimed Tommy. "What are these things moving around?"

"I'm not sure," Dr. Whyze answered, "but I'm going to find out."

Dr. Whyze, a devoted research scientist, had removed a cigarette from a pack with the company logo in bold red letters: WDC. In the microscope he could see the tobacco pieces through the thin paper covering. That's where he spotted something shocking. The small particles of tobacco were moving, independent of each other. Thousands of them rushed about like an army of ants with an important job to do.

Dr. Brian Whyze and his family lived in the city of Notaware. Tommy's mom, Miranda, hated that her husband spent so much time in his lab, a small, metal building in their backyard. In fact, she hated it so much that she divorced Dr. Whyze. Tommy's thirteen-year-old brother, Mark, chose to live with his mother and visit his dad sometimes on weekends, but Tommy stayed with his dad. He liked being in the lab, learning new things, spending time exploring adventures in science. Secretly though, Tommy wished his dad would sometimes play video games with him. He didn't want to say so, but he really missed his mother. He wished he could think of a way to bring his family back together.

Dr. Whyze hurried to the storage cabinet to get a special piece of sound equipment. Working quickly, he connected all the wires and handed a set of headphones to Tommy. They were too big, but he managed to get one earpiece in place while the other rested on his shoulder. Dr. Whyze put on his headphones and adjusted the volume, wondering if he could hear anything. Then they heard it... individual pieces of tobacco talking to each other! Dr. Whyze and Tommy could barely believe what they were seeing and hearing. The tobacco bits had strangely shaped bodies with heads, arms, and

feet. They stood in front of a central tobacco figure that put his hand in the air and motioned for silence.

"Hey, everybody listen up," the sickly-looking leader yelled. "My name's Hack. I'm what you would call a drug terrorist. I create terror, fear, and confusion in humans. I run the underground terrorist training camp that meets in the city sewer." His rough, grating voice stopped. Hacking coughs filled the air as he attempted to clear his throat.

After an awkward pause, Hack continued. "Welcome to our war on kids. We hand out a little pleasure and then move in for the kill. It's our mission to trick kids into believing our lies while they're young, so they'll be easy targets when they get older."

The tobacco particles closely surrounding Hack were dressed like soldiers—sloppy soldiers. They had uniforms made of mismatched fabric scraps, strings, and bits of trash. Some had hoods over their faces, with openings for eyes, mouth, and nose. Others wore dirty, tattered headbands made of braided threads. Their stiff posture and eyes that scanned the crowd were the behaviors of bodyguards. The bigger particles had nametags identifying them as Impulsive, Paranoid, Schitzo, Repulsive, Hyper, Obsessive, Crude, Quitter, Cruel, and Lazy. In spite of their shabby uniforms, they all appeared to be strong, experienced fighters, ready for war.

A group of smaller particles gathered far away from Hack. From large tote bags, they unloaded poster boards, bright colored markers, paints, and brushes. They seemed out of place, but the creepy-looking leader was obviously aware of their presence.

Hack was by far the oldest. Though he appeared physically

weak, he spoke and acted like a powerful crime boss. It was obvious that his word was law in this tobacco world and anyone who resisted or challenged Hack would get no mercy.

"Our purpose is to lure kids into our trap and then hold them hostage to addiction," Hack continued. "That's why I'm here today. I want a few of you to join my dedicated friends and me at our next conference. I'm giving you the opportunity to become a proud soldier in our army of drug terrorists. Your boring lives can change from being ignored and laughed at to being powerful like us. We will teach you how to control humans!

"Our plan is simple—Trick, Trap, and Addict humans. The name of last year's conference was Masters of Deception, and believe me, it was a huge success. Some of last year's recruits are out there right now tricking kids left and right. With a few days of training, you'll be doing the same—and MORE! I'm looking for recruits, so who's in?"

Voices rang out from every part of the crowd. "Yes! I want to be a powerful drug terrorist!"

Hack's thin, dry lips curled into a devious smile as he reacted to the crowd's enthusiastic response. "Only those selected by me will become part of the Devious Forces, the strongest troops sent to lure kids into our trap and make them hostages to drugs. Meanwhile, those of you who remain here will have a chance to create your own special kind of destruction in the bodies of humans."

Everyone watched Hack as he walked through the hushed crowd. His bloodshot eyes studied the hopeful faces to detect the most alert—the ones with the best potential to be deceitful. Some felt so bullied by his forceful presence that they would not make eye contact with him. A few shied away from the idea of tricking and attacking kids. They stepped back to give Hack clear passage. Others stepped closer to get Hack's attention in hopes they would be chosen. Hack continued walking through the group, carefully tapping his finger on the chests of this one and that one. He made no effort to discriminate between males and females. Some of the females looked fierce. After choosing hundreds of recruits, his bodyguards gave each one a filthy headband with a big red X stitched on the front. As they put them on, they stepped forward with pride.

"Let's hear a shout-out for our new drug terrorists," Hack called to the crowd. "These recruits will become the powerful Devious Forces that carry out our war on kids!"

His personal Devious Force led them in the chant: "Hurrah! Down with kids. We hate kids. Trick them! Trap them! Addict them!"

When the shouting and applause finally quieted, a faint, feminine voice spoke up from the crowd.

"Hey, it's wrong to hurt kids. Can you find something else for the Devious Forces to do? There are plenty of adults out there making stupid decisions. But kids—they don't know any better. They just follow the examples set by grown-ups."

"That's right," a few opponents in the crowd agreed, shrinking back as they spoke. They wondered if opposing Hack could be a fatal mistake.

Hack smiled broadly at his Devious Forces and then turned his smirking face to the crowd. "Don't waste my time with weak thinking! Like I said, this is war. Many adults are already in the trap of addiction. They're easy. They fell right into our hands. It's the kids that are our challenge. We want 'em when they're young!"

Hack turned his attention back to the recruits. "You are the elite—the prime particles of the pack." They perked up with pride, listening more closely than before.

"You are the advance team of explosives experts. Your addictive smoke will get into human lungs and bloodstreams. You will damage their hearts and have the opportunity to cause all kinds of diseases. You'll burn all right, but think of the humans you'll take out with you!" Hack threw back his head in a fit of wicked laughter that shook his entire body. "Welcome to the war, my comrades!"

From the crowd of those who had not made the cut, Hack heard a faint female voice say, "This is wrong!" Hack's glaring eyes searched for the soft-spoken protester. Hoping to get her to speak up again, he yelled, "If the powerful Devious Forces can get kids to start smoking when they're young, it's almost certain they'll be hooked for life. They'll never get free. The younger the better, I tell you, the younger the better!"

Then he heard the same voice again from within the crowd. "Well, Mr. Hack, I think you're nothing but an angry, resentful old piece of tobacco. Some human probably hurt you and now you're hurting kids to get revenge."

Tommy and his dad had not said anything to each other. They just watched and listened in amazement. Then Tommy turned to his father and asked, "Why do people smoke when they know it's bad for them?" His sad eyes were troubled behind his thick, black-rimmed glasses.

Dr. Whyze put his arm around Tommy's shoulder, "Well, Son,

cigarettes make you feel good for a little while. Some people say smoking relaxes them. What they choose to ignore is what's happening to their hearts, lungs, and brains. All that smoke does a lot of damage."

At that moment, they heard Hack's harsh voice through their headphones. "Kids are smart, but our Devious Forces will trick them into thinking smoking is cool. We'll turn them into little smoking fools," Hack said, letting loose an evil laugh. Then he strutted around holding a cigarette, pretending to smoke.

Tar, one of Hack's commanders, spoke next. "Kids think smoking is OK because they see adults smoking every day. They watch it on TV and movies, but nobody can make them understand how dangerous it is to smoke."

"That's exactly right," Hack said, drawing the attention back to himself. "Kids think smoking makes them look cool." With the cigarette hanging out of his mouth, Hack posed in different positions, like a muscle man, to make his point. He then put on a wig and pranced, swinging his hips to look like a pretty girl. The crowd roared with laughter.

# Tommy Warns Mark

Tommy suddenly jumped down from the stepladder and ran toward the door.

"Where are you going?" his dad asked.

"To tell Mark."

Mark was tall for his age, with red hair and freckles like Tommy. He felt like the nowhere kid—a nobody just lost in the crowd. He was failing in school, had no friends, and couldn't even get in with the wrong crowd. He hated every freckle on his face as much as he hated being laughed at because of his glasses.

Mark had recently noticed a group of kids on the corner near his mother's apartment. Each day after school, they would hang out together and smoke. *I could start smoking,* Mark thought. *If I do what they do, maybe they'll like me.*

Mark found a private place to try his first cigarette. He did not inhale—just puffed on the cigarette and wondered if he could ever really like it. The more he sucked in the smoke, the more he wondered why anyone wanted something that tasted this nasty. All it did was make him dizzy, choke, and cough. *I have to like it,* he thought determinedly, *or I'll never get in with their group.*

One day, Mark got up the nerve to put a pack of cigarettes in his pocket and walk to the corner where the kids hung out. At first, they pretended Mark was invisible, but they noticed when he pulled out a cigarette and lit it up. He had been practicing, hoping to make a good impression.

Then one of them spoke up. "Look at Mark. He doesn't even inhale."

The girls joined in mocking him with their words. "What's wrong, Mark? Can't you inhale?"

"Sure I can," Mark said defensively. He took a long draw and inhaled deeply. Immediately he began to cough, but he kept going until his head began to spin. The smoke in his eyes caused tears that slipped from under his glasses and ran down his cheeks. He felt like everything in his stomach might explode out his mouth.

Awkward laughter and giggles filled the air. "What's wrong, Mark? Can't take it?"

Mark dropped his cigarette on the ground during his coughing fit. Humiliated and embarrassed, his face flamed as red as his hair. He turned his tall, lanky body away from the kids and ran toward home. One of the boys called after him, "Would you look at that? The four-eyed firecracker can't take a little heat."

Reaching the safety of his bedroom, Mark threw himself across his bed. Tears rolled down his face again, but this time they weren't from smoking. He'd just made a fool of himself. He buried his face in his pillow. The words "four-eyed firecracker" echoed in his memory. He couldn't let that happen again. He made up his mind to learn to inhale.

After a few weeks of practice, Mark learned to inhale. In the beginning, it made him sick, but he figured the reward of acceptance was worth the misery. His payoff came slowly, but Mark eventually became a regular with the other young smokers, who discussed trying marijuana.

As Tommy opened the door to leave the lab, his father said, "Mark probably won't listen to you, but you can try. I have tried to talk to him about smoking and the friends he chooses, but he sure didn't listen to me."

Tommy ran as fast as his skinny legs would carry him to where he knew his brother hung out with his new friends. As he came around the corner, he almost crashed into Mark.

"Hey, Tommy, what are you doing?"

Although Tommy was out of breath, his voice was loud and clear. "Put your cigarettes out! It's a trap. You've been tricked. Smoking is really bad for you."

The kids laughed. "What's all the drama?" one boy said. "How can it be bad when it feels so-o-o good?"

"It's a trick! Smoking will ruin your health," Tommy continued. "I heard little pieces of tobacco inside a cigarette talking about hurting kids—hurting you," he said, pointing to the crowd of teens. "There are Devious Forces trained to trick kids just like you. They're drug terrorists who know they are going to burn up, but they don't care because they plan on taking all of you with them."

The kids looked at Tommy and exploded with laughter.

"Ewww! Little tobacco creatures out to get us! We're so scared!" one of the kids mocked. "Don't worry about us, Tommy. We'll keep our eyes open for the bad guys."

A girl stared at her cigarette and squealed, "I see them—a tiny army rushing to get in my body and tear me up!"

"Go home," Mark said, looking embarrassed. "You're getting as weird as Dad."

But Tommy wasn't ready to give up.

"Mark, come look for yourself," he yelled in frustration.

"I don't care about that science stuff, Tommy, none of us do! Now go home." Mark gave his brother a little push.

With his head down and hands jammed in his pockets, Tommy creeped back to the lab.

Mark watched him go, feeling a little guilty and even a bit curious about what Tommy had just told them. Maybe he shouldn't have been so hard on Tommy, but his dad had already nagged him enough about smoking. He didn't need his brother joining in and making him look foolish in front of his new friends. Mark turned back to the group and lit another cigarette.

As Tommy walked, he spoke aloud, but quietly, "I will not be tricked by a smoking stick. Not me!" He began to walk faster, speaking louder, his head held high, "Smoking is not cool. I'm no fool. Not me! I won't be tricked."

Opening the door to the lab, Tommy saw his dad bent over the microscope. Without looking up, his father asked, "How'd it go, Tommy?"

"They all laughed at me, even Mark." He hoped his dad hadn't heard the slight quiver in his voice. Tommy muscled up his emotions. He was proud as he stepped up to the microscope and put on his headphones. He wanted to be like his dad. His dad didn't smoke.

# Hack Unveils Himself

Father and son continued to spy on the tobacco particles in the cigarette. Hack seemed energized with anticipation as he spoke to those in the crowd who were not chosen. His Devious Forces stood proudly beside him.

"Though you were not chosen as members of the Devious Forces, you can still be an important part in the upcoming training conference. Friends that are like family from around the world will join me for this conference. I need some of you to make posters that motivate and welcome my friends."

Tommy and his dad watched as hundreds of particles began painting posters. They used statements that would encourage the trainees and provide lies for them to use.

KIDS ARE SMART, BUT WE CAN TRICK THEM! SMOKING WON'T HURT YOU. TRY DRUGS. ONE TIME WON'T HURT. EVERYBODY DOES IT. TRY IT, YOU'LL LIKE IT.

Looking through the microscope, the minuscule posters appeared gigantic to Tommy's eyes. The poster that read, WE CAN TRICK THEM, made him furious. In anger he blurted out, "That's not true, Dad! Not me! They won't trick me!"

The particle with the faint voice had moved from the back of the crowd to the front, standing close to where Hack was speaking. "Who are these friends you're talking about?" she asked.

Hack recognized her voice, and by the look on his face, it was clear she was getting on his nerves. Hack responded with gruff bluntness, "I will reveal who they are when I'm good and ready, you little twit. You are to make posters," he said, pointing an ugly finger toward her.

She ignored the accusing finger and said, "I think we have a right to know who our posters will welcome."

“Yeah, that’s right,” some of the others agreed.

“All right, all right, I’ll tell you,” Hack blurted out. “My family members will be there— Slur, Brew and Stumble, Crack, Ready Rock, Blow, Snow, and Big C. We’ll have the big Opiate family from the pharmacy, you know, the pills kids love to steal from their parents. My cousin Spineless will come too, from the Crystal Meth family. You’ll meet Weed, Pot, Wacky Tobakki, Acid, and Optical Illusion. Joining them will be Hug Drug, Brain Damage, Huffy, Sniff, Smack, Speed Freak, the twins Uppers and Downers, and I can’t forget Molly, Bennie, and Roofy. There are many more, but let’s just say, it’s a big family. We are always doing research to develop more drugs for the stupid human species. Our numbers increase every year.”

The bold little female asked, “Why are you so angry, Mr. Hack?”

“I’ll tell you why I’m angry!” Hack shouted, completely out of patience. “When I was a young tobacco leaf, I was part of the premium crop to be used to make the very best cigarettes. A perfect specimen is what they said about me. Quality inspectors said I was ideal. But the owner of the farm didn’t take good care of his fields. Tobacco worms got into our community and began to eat at my outside edges.”

Hack unbuttoned his uniform. It was a gross sight for a piece of tobacco. There were shredded edges, scabs, and burn scars from chemicals used to kill the worms.

“When the farmer found the worms, he sprayed my field with strong pesticides. In the process, he nearly killed me. When the quality inspector came back to the field, he looked at me and said, ‘This plant is damaged. It won’t amount to anything.’ Then he pulled me up by my roots and threw me to the side." Hack hung his head. His shoulders heaved. Sweat dripped from his forehead as he paced back and forth in misery.

Hack raised his face to the crowd again. With a snarl in his voice, he shouted, "I was mad all right! Where did that inspector get off saying I would never be worth anything? The worms and the chemicals did their damage, but I could still have been useful. I could have become chewing tobacco and caused painful cancer of the mouth or turned their teeth yellow."

Hack raised his fist in defiance. "But no-o-o! They decided I was finished, washed up, over! Then I found a way to sneak into the batch of good tobacco being manufactured into cigarettes. Ha! Since then, I've found plenty of ways to get my revenge on humans. That's what I live for—and you're going to help me!"

Hack's ranting brought on another spasm of hoarse coughs. He looked exhausted as he slumped forward and wiped away sweat.

Throughout the crowd small groups discussed whether or not to become a part of Hack's plan. Being in a powerful army to trick humans sounded like a good idea. One at a time, the groups chimed in, "We're with you, Mr. Hack! You can count on us."

Others joined with, "Don't worry, Hack. We got your back." Soon it sounded like a rally with echoes of, "We are terrorists! We will destroy! We hate humans! War on Kids! WOK! WOK! WOK!" Hack began to straighten a bit from his weary, wilted slump.

When the shouting quieted, only one voice was loud and clear. "This is not right," she yelled. "Revenge never produces anything positive, and it will not make you feel better. In the end you will look at the damage you have caused and feel worse than you do now."

She faced the entire group of tobacco pieces, "You should never join forces with someone who is bitter and wants to get revenge. Before long, you'll be full of hate just like him." She turned to weave her way through the crowd to get as far away from Hack as possible. The place was so silent you could have heard a leaf drop.

Hack glared at her as she walked away. With a vicious growl, he yelled, "You turn around and look at me!"

She paused for a second, shaking. She knew Hack was heartless and cruel. She turned around as ordered—not so much because he had ordered it, but more because she was determined not to wilt in fear. At first, she looked down, but thought to herself, *I have nothing to be ashamed of.* She gathered her boldness, straightened to an upright position, raised her eyes, and fixed them on his. The crowd looked on in silence.

"You're not pure tobacco, are you?" Hack asked accusingly. The tense silence had everyone on edge. Frozen, she said nothing.

"I can see it in your color," Hack snarled. "There's something different about you. No wonder you refuse to join us. You're a no-good half weed. I'm an expert on quality tobacco and that's what you're not—you half weed!"

"Very well, if you must know, I'm part ragweed," she replied quietly.

"What did you say!" Hack said with a smirk. "Speak up so everyone can hear you!"

"I'm part ragweed," she repeated loudly, "and I'm not ashamed to say so!"

"You are half weed. I wouldn't want you in my group. Get out of my sight," Hack barked in disgust. "You have no value—you're worthless. Ragweed is one of the lowest plant forms on the earth."

In defense of her species, she said, "I had no control over which family I came from, but that does not make me worthless. I will always be valuable. If we are damaged on the outside, it doesn't make us less valuable. We lose our value when we become bitter and hateful. Maybe you need to think about that. You could choose to forgive those who've hurt you and have a happy life."

"Halfweed, Halfweed, Halfweed!" Hack shook his head and mocked her.

Many in the crowd joined in with crude comments. The tone of their cries said it all. They considered ragweed to be of no value.

She walked through the crowd speaking aloud to herself, "I have nothing to be ashamed of. My genes don't make me worthless. I will not let Hack's words change my opinion of myself. Call me Halfweed if you want. That's who I am and I'm not ashamed!" From that point on, all of the tobacco pieces referred to the brave little fragment as Halfweed—even she herself.

Dr. Whyze, an accomplished scientist, had done research on bacteria found in food and in the atmosphere. Bacteria travels through the air, often causing sickness, similar to the way illegal drugs travel through the body causing diseases. While Tommy watched the tobacco terrorists, the doctor researched how to follow them to the conference. He knew the underworld characters would not want humans to know about their evil activities. But he wanted proof of their destructive plot. He had developed remotely controlled microscopic cameras with built-in microphones. They were similar to cameras that travel through blood vessels, used by surgeons to repair heart damage.

Dr. Whyze thought one of his cameras could follow the drug terrorists through the sewer. He got a monitor from the storage cabinet and set it on the desk beside the microscope. He hurriedly went back to the cabinet and pulled out remote controls, like the ones Tommy used with his games. After he plugged the wires into the monitor, he made one last trip across the room and picked up a small box from the cabinet. Carefully opening it, he used tweezers to lift something from the box. He placed a tiny black object on a glass slide and inserted the slide under another microscope. Tommy could not see what his dad was doing but waited in anticipation. After a few moments, the doctor used the tweezers to move the object to the video microscope.

Dr. Whyze explained to Tommy, "I am placing the camera at the end of the cigarette where the Devious Forces are gathered. This camera is so small it will be unnoticed. It's a long-range lens, so if they get suspicious, I can pull it back from the crowd."

While he was busy hooking up his camera, Halfweed had made her way through the crowd away from Hack. A few sympathizers said comfortingly, "Don't feel bad, Halfweed. A lot of plants are probably mixed breeds."

Others in small groups of four or five smirked at her, "Halfweed! Maybe we should just call her ragweed." Some faked allergic sneezes and coughs to mock her more.

She thought it strange that only the particles in small groups called her Halfweed. Those who stood alone, apart from the group, spoke only words of comfort or nothing at all. If anyone wanted to make fun of her, why not do it as individuals? Why would the mockers speak up only when they were in a group? *They must be cowards*, she thought.

She was deeply hurt because Hack had mocked her in front of the entire crowd. Yet she knew if she became bitter and angry, she would be like Hack—mean and uncaring. She did not want to be like Hack! She made a decision not to let the hurt push her into bitterness and anger.

Her mind was racing with questions. *What should I do? Hack is not right. Is there anything I can do?* She racked her brain. *I am only one small particle. I am also half weed, so maybe I am worthless.* Hopelessness and depression were slowly creeping into her attitude. She wondered, *What will happen if I try to stop Hack? Will anyone help me? I cannot stop hundreds of Devious Forces. Will the crowd laugh at me if I stand against evil? Even if they do, it doesn't matter!*

Halfweed made her decision and said aloud to herself, "If I have to stand alone, I will!" She looked around. "I know there are other half weeds, and it doesn't matter what they are mixed with. Half weeds may be different, but we have our own unique abilities. We are all valuable."

Father and son returned to the microscope to watch the plan unfold. Hack looked up and around every few minutes. Dr. Whyze wondered if he might be aware that someone was watching.

Hack strutted through the crowd. "We will go our separate ways now and most of you will probably never see me again. Some human will pick up this cigarette, light it, and take a big drag. Some of you will become sacrifices, but not all is lost. Others will be doing your part to destroy someone's body. You can all be proud of yourselves."

As Hack waved, a whisper rippled through the crowd and became a loud chant, "Hold humans hostage, especially kids." Hack, his guards, the poster makers, and the new Devious Forces made their exit through the end of the cigarette. Hack thought, *I'm the great escape artist! If someone lights that cigarette now, we're safe and won't go up in smoke.* Halfweed and a few other particles were the only ones that did not join the cheering when Hack made his grand exit.

# The Eye of the Camera

The doctor grabbed the remote controls and turned a few knobs on the monitor. An adrenaline rush swept through him as he realized he had positioned the camera perfectly. He adjusted the knobs, and the blurred images soon became clear. Sure enough, he could remotely control the microscopic camera to follow the group as they departed from the end of the cigarette. Dr. Whyze and Tommy watched Hack and his followers push and shove each other from under the microscope and trek across the back of the lab table and down the table leg.

"Where are they going, Dad?"

"I have no idea, Son, but Hack said the conference was in the sewer," the doctor answered without moving his eyes from the monitor.

Hack and the gang started down the hallway and turned left into the small bathroom connected to the lab. They went around the rug on the floor to the edge of the toilet. Hack suddenly stopped, too tired and out of breath to go any farther. "I have to rest before we climb this wall." He slid down, more like fell, against the cool edge of the toilet.

After a few minutes, Hack stood to his full height, barked a few messy coughs, and ordered, "Let's go." He seemed to be a bit embarrassed about his weakness and coughs, but he led the way up the side of the enormous toilet bowl. Some tricky maneuvering took them under the toilet seat and to the edge of the big bowl of water.

Hack rested and spoke between coughs, "Something will come soon and give us a ride. We cannot stay in the water very long or we'll dissolve and become useless. We'll just wait around to catch a ride."

While Hack waited with his troops, Halfweed could not be lazy and do nothing. She spoke only to herself, mumbling quietly under her breath. "Hack may try to embarrass me, but no one will stop me from doing the right thing." Giving herself a good talking to was often her way of reasoning things out. Sometimes others overheard and gave her strange looks, but she didn't mind.

By the time Hack left the cigarette, Halfweed had made an important decision. She planned to follow and spy on him, to watch his plan unfold. She wondered if others might follow her, and if they did, where would the journey lead them?

Halfweed made her way back to the crowd. She announced, "I'm going to follow Hack. If I can, I will stop his evil plot. If any of you want to join me, meet me at the exit." Several loud comments rose above the nervous laughter. "Not me, that's just crazy," and "she can't do anything. She's a half-weed female."

When Halfweed arrived at the exit, she found a large group who wanted to come with her. She looked them over and then made a statement. "If you go with me, it will be to do what is right. I warn you, doing the right thing might be dangerous. Hack does not care who he hurts. He has hundreds who will do whatever he tells them. They are like robots. It's as if they have microchips for brains and Hack has programmed them.

"It can be very dangerous to follow someone else's lead without thinking for yourself. If all you want to do is follow the crowd, stay here. Doing the right thing takes guts! If you want to stop Hack, follow me." She turned and walked away, willing to go alone if necessary. By the end of her speech, only ten followed her.

Dr. Whyze's microscopic camera had easily followed Hack's combat-bound group. The terrorists stayed on the edge of the toilet bowl waiting for their ride. They did not know humans were spying on them. They were clueless about Halfweed and her group following them.

The doctor saw his young son's eyes glaring at the movement of tiny particles, and he knew a question was soon to follow.

"Dad, what do they mean by waiting for a ride?" Tommy asked.

"I'm not sure, but it seems they float through the sewer system on human waste and other items that are put into the toilet. If I'm right, they won't be going anywhere until someone flushes the toilet."

"Oh, yuck!" Tommy's face twisted, and his eyes squinted. "That makes me want to barf!"

"Me too, Son! But it seems that Hack and his followers are about the same as human waste. The sewer is exactly where they should be. Stay right here and watch the monitor."

Dr. Whyze left the lab and followed the sidewalk into the house.

In the kitchen, he pulled a box of Fruity Critters cereal out of the cabinet. He jerked open a drawer, grabbed a scoop, and hurried back to the lab bathroom. He stood there staring into the toilet bowl. He saw nothing but water, but he knew the particles were there. He poured a scoopful of cereal into the toilet, flushed it, and ran quickly back to the lab.

Tommy's brown eyes had never left the monitor. As his father joined him, they both watched anxiously.

"Wow! You missed it, Dad. When the toilet began to flush, Hack yelled, 'Here's our ride!' Then they all jumped onto those cereal pieces and I heard Hack say, 'This stuff will dissolve quickly, but when we get into the main sewer line, we can catch a more solid ride.' " Tommy put his head in his hands and groaned. "I won't even ask what that means."

"They're afraid of the water," Dr. Whyze responded. "They know if they're in the water too long, they'll disintegrate, which means they will break apart and fade away into nothing."

Just as the camera descended into the water, Tommy noticed in the corner of the monitor that Halfweed was standing on the edge of the toilet rim. She and her little group were catching up with Hack. Tommy pointed and touched the monitor with his finger. "Look, Dad, there's Halfweed. Why is she following Hack?" The camera whisked away after the group of terrorists, leaving Tommy and his father wondering what Halfweed was going to do.

"Hey, Dad, pull back the lens and see what she's doing."

"No, Tommy, we can't lose track of the drug terrorists."

As it turned out, Halfweed and her ten recruits were not far behind Hack. Unnoticed by Tommy and Dr. Whyze—and Hack's forces—they caught rides on the last Fruity Critters going down with the water. Halfweed looked up and saw the microscopic camera floating in the water just before she and her supporters flowed down the pipe to the sewer line.

Hack and his group of drug terrorists were so focused on their mission that they seemed not to notice anything unusual. Hundreds of Devious Forces rode their disintegrating Fruity Critters into a larger sewer line. The secret camera followed close behind. When they arrived in the large sewer line, they saw water filled with all kinds of debris—rides paradise! Bits and pieces of human waste, ruined food, fabric pieces, cigarette butts; anything flushed down toilets, put through kitchen sinks, or drained from city streets was theirs for the taking.

Water, garbage, and sludge from both sides of the pipe flowed into the sewer, bouncing the particles around like rapids of a fast-flowing river. Human waste and other strange things kept pushing them. Without warning, they flew over a huge waterfall into a large pool of water. Popping to the surface, everyone scrambled to stay afloat on anything they could grasp. Hack looked around the enormous pipe as the camera above their heads caught all the action.

Tommy and the doctor laughed as they watched them navigate through the slime-covered pieces of gunk that could easily knock them off their cereal boats.

Hack and his Devious Forces traveled for a long distance. The journey in such a large sewer system was dangerous. They skillfully trudged through giant pipelines, making sure they did not fall into the water and disintegrate.

The walls had billboards that looked similar the ones on the streets of Notaware. The difference was that male and female rats posed with cigarettes hanging out of their mouths, trying to look like famous models. Some dressed like professionals while others displayed their gang colors. Each model had an exaggerated expression of power and control.

Sewer rats, cockroaches, centipedes, and other creatures made their way along the walls and edges of the pipe, staying out of the water. They stopped and watched the proud fleet of unusual boats in their struggle to stay afloat. Small groups of sewer rats, all smoking and wearing their gang colors, acknowledged Hack as though they knew him, yet they seemed to be afraid of him. They removed trash that might interfere with Hack's passage, then stepped back and nodded respectfully.

Finally, the terrorists arrived at a box-like, concrete open area that had pipes coming from all sides. Hack ordered his army to get off their rides so they could dry out and rest. They climbed to the outer corners, crowded but safe.

A time of rest gave the Devious Forces the opportunity to ask questions: "Where are we? How much farther is it?" One asked a more personal question. "Hack, the sewer rats all seem to recognize you, but apparently they won't challenge you. What's the deal with that?"

"In the past, the sewer rats controlled everything in the underworld," Hack replied. "They were bigger and stronger than all other underworld creatures. So when my friends and I planned a conference, we knew we had to take control."

"But how?" one asked.

Hack's dry, cracked lips curved into a self-approving smile. "We set traps for rats, somewhat like the traps we set for the human species. I knew if we could get them addicted to drugs, we could control their lives. We are very small, but when we get into their bodies, we take over their minds. The different gangs of rats think they're tough, but we control them. We let them survive, but any drug user is our servant."

"Why did the rats start smoking?" one asked.

Slightly amused at the question, Hack pointed to the billboards and grunted. "We tricked them! We put up those big signs, and they just started smoking. They believed it would make them like the rats in the pictures. The first time they breathed in the smoke, they coughed and gagged just like the humans. They kept sucking the nicotine into their lungs until they were hooked. The rats, generally a hyperactive species, grew to enjoy the calm feeling. When the effect of the nicotine was gone, they always came back for more. It didn't take long for tobacco to cause cancer in the small rats, and many of them died painful deaths. Even so, those who lived would gather up cigarette butts to smoke. Rats walking around puffing on cigarettes look just as dumb as humans."

"Did it bother you to trick them?" Schitzo asked.

"No," Hack scoffed. "They are just rats, and it's the same with humans."

"Well, does tricking humans bother you?"

"No! I figure that if a species is dumb enough to smoke cigarettes, they deserve what they get. It's not my fault. I remind you, it's their own dumb decisions."

Hack went on with the chilling tale of the rats. "We can trap as many rats as we want and repeat the addiction process forever. A few of them had enough sense to stay away from the trap, but like people, rats are curious and want to experience the calmness that nicotine provides." Hack pointed to a group of rats. One was lying down, gasping for air.

"There's one. They're watching him die. That's what we do, kill 'em. I love it! You would think the human species would be smarter than rats, but some just have to try it. They keep us in business. When we get to the conference, I'll point out the crack rats. We use them like slaves."

"What is a crack rat?" a tobacco particle named Tar asked.

"A crack rat is a cocaine-addicted rat—a real sight to see! You'll love it. We put crack in their food and cigarettes and they were addicted immediately. They'll do anything for more crack. OK, you guys," Hack ordered. "Time to roll. Follow me."

"Hack doesn't care who he hurts! He's evil!" Tommy shouted in anger. In desperation, he thought of Mark and the other kids. "Dad, what can we do?"

"We will follow Hack and his Devious Forces, learn their techniques, and then go from there. Knowledge equals success if you do the right thing with it. Maybe we can warn kids and adults about this evil."

Halfweed halted her recruits to rest whenever Hack and the Devious Forces stopped to rest. They hid close enough to hear their conversations and were infuriated to hear the story of cruelly tricking the rats. Her little group of followers recognized what Halfweed had known for some time. Hack, just like drugs, had no conscience and was cold and calculating. He would try to destroy anything or anyone who got in his way.

She looked at her small group and asked, "Do you want to be terrorists that destroy kids?" One by one, they answered with bold-sounding voices, "Nope, not me!" From that moment on, they named themselves Nopers. They declared, "We are Nopers, not Dopers."

Halfweed gave each of them a name that reflected positive behavior qualities: Rebound, Curious, Tenacity, Tender Heart, Perceptive, and Courageous. She vigorously encouraged her troops. "We must stop these killers who cause cancer and promote the destruction of kids. They are friends of addictive drugs, but not our friends. We are definitely in a war."

"What do we do? How can we stop them?" one of Halfweed's followers asked. He was thinking of the lack of support from other tobacco particles, who would rather be drug terrorists than Nopers.

"I'm not sure," Halfweed said, "but one thing I know, we must get into that conference to see their plan." Pointing her finger upward in the direction of Hack's group, she continued. "See that black box above the water? That, my friends, is a camera. A human has been watching Hack since he and his recruits started their trip. I have made it a point to stay behind the camera so it can't see us, but maybe the human can help us."

Curious fearfully commented, "Maybe the human uses drugs. Some humans are heartless just like Hack. They don't care who they hurt and might try to destroy us."

"We will have to take that chance." Halfweed sounded braver than she felt.

They watched a cricket try to avoid getting wet, jumping from one side of the water to the other. As he jumped, he struck the camera that hovered overhead. Splash! The camera hit the nasty water. They watched it float underneath a piece of fabric. Halfweed held her breath and waited for the camera to reappear, but nothing happened. The wet fabric was too heavy, and the remote-controlled camera was trapped in the water.

# Disappearance of the Underworld

The screen suddenly went blank. They could not see or hear anything. It was as if the underworld had vanished. Was this one of Hack's tricks?

Panicked, Tommy asked in a soft, high-pitched voice, "Dad, what happened?"

Silence answered Tommy's question as Dr. Whyze nervously kept adjusting knobs, trying to make something happen. All they could hear were unidentified noises.

The minuscule camera that had traveled unnoticed by Hack's group was now somewhere under the water, a short distance behind them. Halfweed knew it would soon float past Hack to the main sewer and be lost forever. She wanted human witnesses to see the evil plot that Hack and his terrorists planned to carry out.

Halfweed addressed her recruits. “I have to save the camera!” The Nopers stepped forward, willing to take the risk with her.

“No!” She held her hand up, shook her head, and said sternly, “It’s too dangerous. I want you all to wait here.”

Looking into the water, Halfweed tried to figure a way to catch the camera as it floated downstream. She bravely jumped onto a floating object and raced forward. As she sped along, she caught a glimpse of Hack and the terrorists standing by the water, waiting for a ride.

One of them spotted her. “Hey, look! There goes Halfweed.” Not believing it, Hack looked up. He watched with amazement as she jumped from one piece of debris to another. He quickly pointed to five terrorists, ordering them to catch her and throw her in the water. “Don’t come back until the job is done!” he shouted.

Hack’s expertise in the underworld helped him spot a good ride. He hopped onto an ice cream stick as it floated by. His bodyguards followed and rode along beside him. The new Devious Forces remained to fend for themselves. If they fell in the water and disintegrated, Hack did not care.

Hack’s terrorists paddled fast to catch Halfweed. They caught up with her just as she grabbed the piece of fabric that covered the camera. She tugged at the edge, trying to free the camera. She was startled when Hack’s followers jumped onto the fabric.

“What are you doing here?” one of the drug terrorists yelled.

“None of your business,” she answered. *Are the Nopers safe?* she wondered. *Or did Hack send his scum warriors after them?*

"We were told to find out what you're doing, then throw you in the water so you'll disintegrate."

Halfweed was unsure what to say. She knew she could not fight all five of them. *Can I negotiate with them or talk them into changing their minds about working for Hack? Can I convince them to help me?* she asked herself.

"What are you trying to pull?" one of her enemies asked. "Tell us or we'll throw you in the water right now!" Closing in on her, they grabbed and pushed her to the edge of the fabric.

"Wait! Wait just a minute. Let me ask you some questions, and then you can do as you wish."

"You're really not in any position to ask us anything, are you?" they responded. "But go ahead, ask your questions. Then you can answer ours."

"OK, you've got yourself a deal. Why are you here to get me?"

"Hack told us to catch you, to see what you're up to and get rid of you."

"Why does Hack want to hurt me? I've done nothing to him."

"Look, ragweed, we just do what we're told."

"He wants to hurt kids. Don't you realize how wrong that is?" she asked, still unable to understand such cruelty.

"Humans hurt him and he wants to get even," they answered like programmed computer chips. "We want to help him."

"Does that make sense to you? Can't you think for yourselves?"

She wondered, *is that confusion I see on their puzzled faces?* "Hack is a bitter old tobacco particle, and his bitterness has blinded him to common sense. You must learn to think for yourselves and decide between right and wrong. Think about where you're going before you follow anyone, especially someone who is angry."

A shaky voice answered, "Everyone was following Hack, and all those tobacco particles can't be wrong!"

Halfweed responded boldly, "You're wrong! Not everyone followed Hack. I sure didn't and you want to know why? It's because I know how to think for myself. I know what he's asking us to do is wrong."

Looking bewildered, one asked her, "What should we do?"

Halfweed knew the right choice but did not tell them. She wanted each one to make a personal choice. A Noper had to be trusted to do what was right, not just follow the loudest voice in the crowd.

Holding tightly to Halfweed, the five terrorists whispered behind her back.

"If we don't throw her in the water like Hack ordered, he'll come after us next."

"But she's right about him. What he's doing is wrong."

"I don't care. You can't always do the right thing."

"Yeah, sometimes you have to follow the crowd."

One of them confessed, "I never did like what Hack was doing. I think I just got caught up in all the excitement. Truthfully, I've been wondering how to get out of this."

"You coward!" one of them lashed out.

"Whatever, but I'm choosing to walk away. I'm not willing to follow the crowd when I know they're wrong."

Another particle turned and spoke to Halfweed. "So, what are you doing here?"

"I'm just trying to stop Hack's evil work."

In shock, they asked, "Alone? That's impossible. His troops won't stop until you're history."

"We all have to stand up for what's right, and sometimes that means standing alone. It's the only way to grow stronger."

Two of the terrorists decided to help Halfweed. Not backing down from the others, she stared into the eyes of one terrorist and asked, "Are you going to do the right thing, or follow the crowd?"

"I'm following Hack," he answered with no shame, as though there were no other answer. Then she moved to the next particle. "And you?" she asked.

"I'm going to follow Hack too," the voice came back.

When she looked into the third particle's eyes, he said "Hack," before she could even ask.

Halfweed was shocked that, when faced with the truth, they still made the wrong choice. They had followed Hack without thinking for themselves and were about to do it again. It was as if they had a fortress built around their minds and they couldn't get free. They simply ignored the truth. She wondered if she could really depend on the other two. *Would they weaken and follow Hack?*

"What will you do?" she asked them. She had not told them about her few followers or about the camera snagged under their feet. She wanted her two possible converts to make the right choice even though they knew the odds were against them.

Because of Halfweed's bravery, one of the two spoke firmly, "I choose to do what is right. I'm going with her."

"Me too," the other said. "I want to do the right thing."

The three Hack patriots stepped back and glared at the traitors. "Hack will destroy you for this."

Halfweed was encouraged that two of Hack's former followers had decided to do the right thing. She was fully aware that the three still siding with Hack were the weaklings. Moving forward confidently, she demanded, "Get off now, or we will throw you off!" The three weaklings, trying to look tough, moved to the edge of the fabric and jumped to the sewer pipe.

"This is a big mistake," they threatened. "You'll be hearing from us!" They waited at the edge of the water for Hack and the rest of the terrorists to float by.

Halfweed and her two newest Nopers wasted no time. When Hack's followers were out of sight, she informed the pair of their group's name, the Nopers. She led them in a pledge, always to say nope to dope and kid terrorism. They took off their terrorist headbands, and she instructed them to grab the edge of the fabric. "Now pull it up," she shouted. The three of them tugged with all their might. Her two recruits were clueless why they were pulling, but they did as she instructed. Halfweed saw the camera float free and bounce up. It splashed wildly in the water, then rose like magic to the top of the pipe.

"What is that thing?" one of the new Nopers yelled in fear.

Halfweed calmly replied, "It's a camera controlled by humans. It's been following Hack and his army through the sewer. I don't know how many humans are watching, who they are, or what they want. But I think maybe they can help us."

The camera finally slowed its erratic movement and paused as though it were looking for something. The front of it turned up, down and then in a circle. It finally stopped and focused on the three Nopers watching it.

Tommy and Dr. Whyze were thrilled when the screen flickered back to life. A few adjustments made the blurry picture clear. While Dr. Whyze tried to figure out the exact location of the camera, Tommy hopped to attention and yelled, "Whoa, Dad, it's Halfweed! Who are those two with her?"

"I don't know."

"Where are Hack and his group?" Tommy asked.

"I have no idea. We will follow Halfweed and try to figure out what's happening."

They watched as the trio of Nopers floated on the piece of fabric.

"We have to find a place to hide," Halfweed told them. "Hack and his followers are not far behind us. They'll be looking for us."

She instructed the Nopers to follow her. They jumped to the walls of the pipe and climbed until safely hidden behind some crinkled gum wrappers. They waited quietly for Hack and his team to float by so they could follow them. In the distance, they saw Hack and his terrorists. They could hear him barking orders, "Find them! Look behind every piece of garbage. Don't you dare miss any possible hiding place!"

The Devious Forces jumped off their ride and scurried up the walls of the pipe. They looked under and behind every stinking scrap they could reach. There were hundreds of them looking for Halfweed and the two traitors. The three that had failed to capture Halfweed were riding with Hack. They had informed him of their failure and that two of his terrorists had decided to become Nopers.

"You failed!" Hack screamed, shaking his fist at the three terrorists. "You are not worthy to be in the Devious Forces." The three trembled, knowing what their fate might be.

"Throw them off," he said in disgust. "They don't deserve a chance to work with us in the war against kids. I hope they dissolve in the water." His angry tirade sent him into a coughing spasm.

Hack's bodyguards rushed toward the three frightened terrorists who were now trying to escape the inevitable. They jumped to the wall of the pipe just as the bodyguards pushed them.

"Don't come back, you cowards!" their angry words echoed through the pipes.

The escapees ran away as fast as they could, constantly glancing behind, hoping no one followed. Soon they were far away from Hack and his Devious Forces.

While Hack and his troops were distracted, Halfweed decided it was time to make a break for it. She knew it was only a matter of time until they were discovered. Motioning to the Nopers with her arm in the air, she led the way. The small group began to run and hop from one pile of rubble to the next.

# THE EVIL FAMILY

## Halfweed Is Captured

Halfweed looked as far ahead as possible, desperately searching for an escape route. Voices of terrorists that echoed through the pipe suddenly became quiet. Halfweed and her Nopers were shocked when Hack's soldiers caught up with them. There was no way out—they were captured. Hundreds of terrorists closed in and the ugly sneers on their faces frightened the Nopers. Halfweed knew that giving up was not an option. Fear made her freeze perfectly still, but her eyes kept looking for a way out.

They were near the entrance of the conference center and all three Nopers watched the admission process. An attendant at the door allowed only those with ID badges to enter. They glanced nervously at the circle of drug terrorists surrounding them. Halfweed was worried, but her two followers were way past worried. They shook like tobacco leaves in the wind. Hack arrived, wheezing and gasping for air, his lethal glare fixed intently on Halfweed.

Hack finally caught his breath enough to speak. "You two," he pointed to his ex-followers standing with Halfweed, "have betrayed your purpose and joined a do-gooder who thinks she's better than us. Our responsibility is to cause addiction and disease in human bodies. You are traitors to the entire underworld! We will throw you in the water with Halfweed. You'll decompose and rot along with her."

Halfweed was determined to be strong, so she reacted quickly, "You know what you are doing is wrong! Your bitterness is controlling you. You should help humans, not hurt them."

Hack shot back, "I have helped humans make money!"

Halfweed was not fooled by his talk of help. "Yeah, you sure helped them, Hack. You've helped the selfish, greedy humans who don't care how much their poisons hurt others."

"So what!" Hack responded.

Shaking her head in pity, Halfweed said, "Your hatred has made you blind, Hack."

Tar was ready for action. "Let's throw 'em in the water!"

The eager drug terrorists reached out for the Nopers. "Yeah, throw the traitors in with the rest of the garbage where they belong. Get rid of them!"

Halfweed's voice hurled back, "You may destroy us, but someday your cruel plans will be exposed. You are totally evil. You, and all of your drug friends, are lower than the sewer—the scum of the earth!"

Hack's crew erupted in frenzied protest. "Call it evil if you wish, but that is our purpose—and we love our jobs! We destroy kids, families, anyone we can." Their fists punched the air while they screamed, "WOK, WOK, WOK. War on Kids, War on Kids, War on Kids!"

Hack, furious that he had lost two of his workers, looked at his bodyguards and ordered, "Tie up these three and take them to the holding cell. Five of you guard the door, and you other five come with me."

Five terrorists grabbed Halfweed and her two Nopers. They tied and dragged them to a small room out of sight from the crowded entrance. After they forced their captive Nopers into a cell, the five guards arranged themselves in a line outside the door.

# Hack Meets with Other Corrupt Leaders

Hack and his bodyguards walked defiantly down the pipe toward a private meeting room. Terrorist drug leaders sat around a large table, waiting for him to arrive. In a far corner were a few low-ranking terrorists and sickly crack rats. They were slaves who did only what they were told. Those around the table were commanders who represented both legal and illegal drugs: Crack, Cocaine Powder, Heroin, Hash, Prescription Sedatives, Tobacco, Marijuana, Alcohol, Methamphetamines, and many more. They were the power players, the enforcers who made all decisions in the drug underworld. None of them had any guilt about developing the best plan of addiction for their particular drug. There was no jealousy or competition among them. They worked as a team to trap as many humans as possible. If one drug did not get them, maybe another would.

While waiting for Hack, they enjoyed each other's horrible stories and watched videos of humans who had died from overdoses. They would double over with laughter when a drunk driver caused a wreck and killed or crippled another person, especially kids. Teens

who were killed while drinking and driving caused them to swell with pride. Teen suicide brought them to their feet with wild cheers and high fives. Oh, what pleasure when a pregnant woman took drugs and gave birth to an addicted baby. If the little screaming thing lived, they knew it would most likely become an adult drug addict. They loved it when a human went to prison on drug-related charges or a family broke up because of their efforts.

Hack posted his bodyguards outside and strutted into the room. The commanders welcomed him with enthusiasm. "You're late.

Where have you been, Hack?" a voice asked from the table.

"I had a little problem with a female do-gooder. She decided to follow us to the conference center and nose around. She convinced two of my Devious Forces to join her little band of failures. We have never had traitors," Hack said, continuing his rant. "They've named themselves the Nopers. She's nothing but a mixed breed of tobacco and ragweed. I even gave her a special name, Halfweed. Guards are keeping them in the holding cell. I thought we should decide as a group what to do with them."

Brain Damage, known in the stores as paint thinner, answered without hesitation, "Force them to inhale me. I'll eat their brains, drive them crazy, and then leave them to die alone."

Smack suggested, "I could overdose them and take care of that for you."

Opiate chuckled. "Let the rats eat them. They'll be reduced to rat poop."

Weed yelled out, "I've got it! Get our camera crew to take pictures of them to show at the conference as an illustration of what happens to traitors. We can wipe them out when we are finished with them."

Hack liked that suggestion. "Great idea! Do we all agree?" The leaders voiced unanimous approval.

Hack motioned to a terrorist standing in the corner with the rats. "Get the camera crew to shoot some pictures of the traitors." The obedient slave left the room to relay Hack's plan.

The camera crew, comprised entirely of tobacco terrorists,

picked up the equipment and went to the holding cell. The chief operator growled viciously at the Nopers, "You sorry bunch of losers. You betrayed your own family."

The prisoners remained silent while the camera crew mocked and filmed them. Halfweed stared at the camera and noticed it looked like a smaller version of the remote camera that was following them.

# STUPID FOLLOWS STUPID

## Halfweed Crashes the Conference

Dr. Whyze aligned the remote camera to hover over the action so he and Tommy could watch. They were not able to see into the cell, but they knew Halfweed and her Nopers were inside.

"Dad, we have to help Halfweed! She's trying to do what's right. She has no one else." His voice rose in despair.

"I know, Son, but I'm not sure what to do."

The three terrorists who had failed to capture Halfweed feared being caught by Hack. They trudged cautiously up the side of the pipe and were shocked when suddenly met by a group of Nopers. The frightened terrorists told them that two of Hack's Devious Forces went with Halfweed, but all were probably captured and destroyed.

One of the terrorists exclaimed, "They will destroy you, too, if you continue to follow her!"

"Yes, but our destruction will be for trying to do what is right, so we are not turning back. We will find out what happened to her. We are not terrorists, we are Nopers."

The ten Nopers propelled their craft through the nasty liquid, staying alert for terrorists as they searched for Halfweed. Tenacity, named for his tireless determination, jumped to a solid edge of pipe and motioned for the others to follow. They saw the five guards standing in front of an opening in the wall.

"What do we do now? Do you think Halfweed is in that room?" they asked each other.

Doctor Whyze was surprised when Tommy reached for the camera's controls. His young son normally would not touch any of the equipment without asking for permission.

"What are you doing, Tommy?"

"I'm going to show them where Halfweed is."

Tommy made the camera move slowly up the pipe directly over the Nopers who were huddled behind debris discussing their next move. He dropped the camera into the middle of the group. Startled, they jumped back. Then seeing what the object was, they watched as it slowly rose to the ceiling and then down the pipe over the heads of the terrorists guarding the cell door. Tommy carefully turned one of the control knobs in a circle causing the camera to turn slowly like a ceiling fan.

"Hey, I think the human is trying to send us a message," Tenacity said, taking charge. "Halfweed might be in the room where those guards are standing. I think we can take them. After all, there are ten of us to their five. Let's make a new boat big enough so you can hide behind trash we pile on top of it. We'll move toward them like I'm alone. When we get close, then we go for it. If Halfweed is in the room, we will rescue her."

They pulled a big piece of orange peel from the water. Working quietly, they gathered paper, food particles, and other trash to build a wall down the middle of the rind. The pile of trash was wide and tall enough to hide behind. They managed to find some strong thread to tie up their enemies.

"What if she's not there?" Curiosity asked.

"Well, maybe we can make them tell us where she is."

"Everybody be quiet. Don't say a word," Tenacity whispered.

Working as a team, Halfweed's rescuers cautiously slid the peel back into the stream of water and jumped on. Tenacity stood alone in plain sight while the others crouched behind the wall they had built. Their little raft floated near the guards, who came to attention and gazed at the lone tobacco particle approaching them.

When the group of Nopers got close enough to the guards, Tenacity shouted, "Go!" Everyone jumped off at the same time and quickly closed in on the five unsuspecting guards. The Nopers were gaining control.

Hearing the loud commotion, the camera crew hurried from the cell to film the invaders. But the Nopers quickly grabbed the crew and dragged them back into the cell. They untied Halfweed and the two other Nopers, then securely bound the guards and camera crew. Their captives were red-faced with anger and shame, already fearful of Hack's response.

Thrilled to be untied, Halfweed hugged her friends and welcomed the two new recruits. They huddled in a corner of the room and discussed what they should do next.

Halfweed asked, "How did you know I was here?"

"While we were trying to find you, the human dropped the camera down where we could see it—scared us half to death! Then we noticed the camera moved in a circle over the heads of a couple of Hack's Devious Forces. We guessed the camera must be signaling your location."

Halfweed jumped up, hurried out the door of the cell, and looked up. Sure enough, there was the camera. She turned and walked back into the room.

"That camera has followed Hack from the very beginning, and I am convinced the human watching us is our friend. Don't go bonkers on me, but I believe the human wants to help us."

After a brief pause, waiting for outbursts of objections, she continued, "Thirteen Nopers is a very small force when compared to our enemy dopers, numbering in the thousands. There is no way we can overthrow them; however, I may have a plan that will work. If we can get that camera into the conference room," she said, pointing to the door leading outside, "the humans will see Hack's ugly scheme and warn the kids."

"That humongous thing is so much bigger than the conference center's camera that the terrorists can't help but notice. I don't think that will work, Halfweed," Cautious said.

"I am willing to take that chance." She eyed the terrorists' camera on the floor, pointed to the captured crew chief, and said, "Untie him and give him his camera."

Halfweed motioned for the other Nopers to stand behind her. Bravely instructing the terrorist to film her, she looked directly into the lens and began to speak.

"Hack, you and your terrorists are totally evil. You take pleasure in destroying innocent lives. You operate in the sewer because you are sewage, real slime. Behind me, you see fellow Nopers who have joined with me to expose you. We will not rest until kids everywhere recognize that you are their enemy. We may die in our effort, but it is worth it to save the children. You will not stop us. When kids begin to mock and ignore you, you will know that it started with one strong Noper who told others the truth. Then they told someone else, who told another, and it will continue." Pointing into the camera, she shouted, "YOU, and your slithering helpers, will be exposed for the evil terrorists you are!"

Halfweed stopped speaking and gave a signal to turn off the camera. A slow, confident smile spread across her face as she ordered, "Give me the master disk!"

She handed the new video to a Noper, "Keep this. We may need it later. Now, tie up the scum. Get their ID badges and their uniforms."

Halfweed walked out of the room to the edge of the stream. She stared into the water, watching small puddles of cooking oil float on top. "Everyone scoop up enough oil to coat yourselves then put on the guards' uniforms."

"Why?" asked Curiosity.

"I don't have time to explain, just do it!" They obeyed Halfweed as she slathered herself with cooking oil and reached for a terrorist's headband.

"Don't miss a spot. It's important to cover yourselves completely. You'll understand later." Some gagged as they coated themselves in smelly, slimy oil and put on the dirty headbands that belonged to the terrorists.

Pointing toward six Nopers, she ordered, "You six stay here as guards. Five of you stay outside the room and one inside. Make sure you keep the captives quiet. If Hack looks this way, he will see five guards assigned to watch me. Seven of us have ID tags from the guards and film crew. If the human will help us, we are going to take this camera into the middle of the conference. We can help film Hack's strategy of corruption and expose his plan to destroy innocent children. The human will have the video to prove what he is up to."

The six Nopers looked at each other in wide-eyed fear. Finally, one shaky voice asked, "Are we going into their conference?"

"Yes," Halfweed boldly answered. "We are going into the middle of the crowd. We will be surrounded by thousands of Devious Forces, but they will think we are terrorists just like them."

Not convinced her plan would work, a soft voice asked, "How do we explain the big camera?"

"Simple. We tell them it's the newest technology and hope that will impress them." Halfweed paused, looked steadily at each one individually, and thought, *Will one of them defect and, out of fear, go back to Hack?*

She continued. "OK, Nopers, let's find out if the human operating this camera will help us." Walking out of the room, Halfweed looked up and motioned for the human to lower the camera.

Tommy still had the controls. "What do I do, Dad?" he asked.

Dr. Whyze watched the screen closely. "Do what they want."

Tommy lowered the camera right to the edge of the water where Halfweed waited. When the camera came within her reach, she swung into action.

"I want three of you on each side of the camera," she instructed. "When a good ride comes along, we will get on it and navigate to the entrance of the conference. Ignore those who are checking entry passes. Follow me and do what I tell you."

A large piece of cardboard approached from upstream. They caught it and struggled to maneuver the big, heavy camera onboard. Tommy was able to help them by raising it with the controls. Halfweed stepped to the front as they started their journey to the conference room.

Nearing the conference entrance, they spotted a couple of particles chatting casually as they checked IDs. Most of the terrorists were already in the conference center. The little Nopers on their cardboard boat were more afraid than ever. No one said it, but they all wondered where Hack was. He would recognize them. They knew their mission was crucial and there was no turning back. Halfweed motioned for them to unload the camera at the entrance. She stepped off her ride and paid no attention to those checking entrance passes.

In a deep voice, not sounding at all like Halfweed, she shouted, "Stand back. The film crew is coming through."

The chatterboxes stepped back, allowing Halfweed and her followers to pass. Their loud conversation faded to a soft hum as some of them curiously eyed Halfweed.

"Hey, isn't that the half weed that defied Hack?" someone asked.

"It looks like her, the one with the ragweed mix," another answered.

"Oh, you two are always looking for trouble. Besides, when you've seen one half weed, you've seen 'em all."

"Well, I guess you're right. They're all the same," he answered.

"What's the deal with the big camera?" one asked.

"Latest technology," responded Curiosity as they walked toward the entrance.

The group entered the conference center, relieved that they were not stopped. There were thousands of terrorists representing every kind of drug. Some were seated, anxious for the conference to begin, while others mingled, laughed, and visited.

Hack's poster crew busily hung the posters they had prepared. The one over the main platform said: "Welcome to The Annual WOK Conference." Smaller letters at the bottom of the sign read "War on Kids."

Halfweed looked around, unsure of where to put the big camera. She hoped no one noticed her hesitation. She saw projectors mounted on the ceiling of the auditorium and muttered to herself, "this

could be a problem." She caught a glimpse of a platform at the back of the room that looked like a control booth and motioned for her Nopers to set up the camera in the booth. She immediately began to study the lighted control boards. ON-OFF-PAUSE. *Simple enough,* Halfweed thought, breathing a sigh of relief. She would be able to operate the projectors in case someone told her to start or stop a video.

The crowd began to move toward their seats for the conference to start. Around the outside walls, tables were set up for the attendees to pick up their favorite T-shirts. Shirt logos were the same as the posters that wallpapered the arena. The most popular one was "TTA," in large fluorescent letters, with "Trick, Trap and Addict" spelled out below in smaller lettering. Another said "Hold Humans Hostage," and written in smaller letters underneath, "Especially Kids." The atmosphere was electric with excitement, like a rock concert and political rally all in one. Music blared in the background, and poster makers proudly carried their signs around the arena.

Built of trash from the streets of Notaware, along with garbage and food from the sewer, the arena was a nasty place. The main stage curtain was made of stained toilet paper hung from bacteria-covered toothpicks. Long metal strips from tin cans were fashioned into benches. Jumbo video screens, made from dingy white cloth, were mounted high on each side of the stage. Every terrorist had a good view from every angle. Faint light filtered through an overhead drain cover.

Halfweed was unsure if the human could hear or see what was happening. Hundreds of tobacco particles moved around to get better seats. She moved in front of the camera lens and pointed to the left. Relieved, she watched it move in the direction she pointed. Pointing again, this time to the right, she watched the camera follow her directions.

"Can you hear me?" Halfweed spoke to the camera. The front of the camera rocked up and down as though nodding "yes." She covered her mouth to smother a giggle. Her camera crew was still very nervous about the risk they were taking.

Tommy and Dr. Whyze knew it was important to pay close attention to the little creature named Halfweed. Turning to his dad, Tommy blurted out, "Dad, I will never do drugs! No cigarettes, nothing! Not me!" He wanted all the kids in the world to see the video of Halfweed's brave fight against the drug underworld.

Tommy jabbed his fist into the air to emphasize each word and yelled to the monitor, "Hey, Hack, NOT ME!"

# The Conference Begins

Mr. Flatulent, the Master of Ceremonies, entered from the side of the platform. He was dressed in a lopsided top hat and ill-fitting tuxedo made of patched black fabric.

"Welcome. Welcome. Welcome," he shouted into his microphone as he strutted toward the center stage. The spontaneous applause was deafening, drowning the sounds of noisy farts that exploded with each "welcome." Loud music that was out of tune decreased, and the applause stopped. Mr. Flatulent began to speak.

"You have been specially chosen as Devious Forces for the war on kids."

"WOK! WOK! WOK!" the audience chanted enthusiastically.

"I love that sound! WOK! Last year our conference was MOD, M-O-D, Masters of Deception. We are the masters of deception!" he shouted.

"MOD! We're MOD!" others added.

Mr. Flatulent continued, "We remain the masters of deception. That is what we do! That is who we are! And this is war on kids." The crowd roared in agreement.

Mr. Flatulent bellowed like an announcer at a wrestling event. "I want you to welcome our heroes, the organizers of the conference. They are responsible for the destruction of people's lives and health, the devastation of families, and sending many to prison. They have the potential to destroy a country!" He extended his hand outward toward the right side of the stage. The terrorist leaders emerged, waving to the audience as if they were Hollywood stars.

"Here they are!" Mr. Flatulent proudly announced. The audience went wild, jumping and whistling, with loud applause and shouts of admiration. The honored drug leaders waved, bowed, and signaled thumbs up. Flatulent directed them to the only things in the whole auditorium that were sparkling clean—huge, finely decorated gold chairs.

# Professor Virtuoso

"Our first guest has spent his life creating laboratory experiments to discover new drugs," Flatulent said, beginning his introduction. "He will show you how to do the most damage to kids. We call him Professor. He is a master at developing and using drugs. His hatred for kids has driven him to continue his work no matter what the cost."

Pointing to the video control booth, Mr. Flatulent instructed, "Show the picture of Professor Virtuoso before he volunteered to run the lab. I want everyone to understand how much he has sacrificed."

Halfweed pressed the button marked Professor Virtuoso, hoping the right image would come up. A young, healthy, clear-skinned professor filled the screen and wowed the audience.

Extending his hand toward the side of the stage, Flatulent said, "Please, welcome Professor Virtuoso."

The crowd looked away from the screen to the tall particle limping onto the stage, dragging his left leg. They erupted in welcoming applause. *Oh, I get it*, Halfweed thought, *before and after*. His condition was worse than Hack's. Behind glasses holding to the end of his nose, they could see dark, sagging skin under his bloodshot eyes. Many wondered if he had slept in days. Disgusting, oozing scabs covered his skin. His head moved and jerked uncontrollably.

The applause gradually changed to gasps as they stared in horror at the professor. Some of them were so repulsed they looked away. Whispers rippled through the onlookers.

"I don't mind if drugs destroy humans, but drugs have destroyed one of our own family," said someone. Others sadly agreed.

Professor Virtuoso's voice was weak and trembling. "Humans! What a strange species—always looking for a new high. Some of them are so stupid they never give a second thought to how drugs will damage them." Most of them never consider that they will become addicted and destroy their lives." His coughs produced gooey, yellow phlegm that he spit on the floor. "I volunteered to do this job two years ago. I take the drugs so I will know the best way to help humans destroy themselves. Some of them will end up just like me."

A slight twinkle in his bloodshot eyes left no doubt that he enjoyed his murderous occupation. His speech pattern changed back and forth from slow to rapid. Some words were so slurred that the audience strained to understand what he was saying. He paused, looking from side to side as though he were lost. The audience waited quietly.

"Oh, yeah!" he said, remembering where he was. "The drugs have ruined some of my brain cells, but it's worth it to create drugs that appear to help, not hurt. Kids will try them and completely lose control of their stupid little lives. Drugs will slowly eat away their minds and bodies like a rat scratching away at their brains." His fingers wiggled above his head to demonstrate. "Until, finally, they are just like me."

While the audience went wild with cheers and applause, the professor motioned to a group of addicted slave rats. The poor rats were so malnourished you could see through transparent skin that had lost most of its fur. They looked old, weak, and sickly because drug addiction was slowly killing them.

"Bring out a virtual model," he said as loudly as his weakened voice allowed. The opening curtain revealed a human replica seated in a chair. The slave rats struggled to pull and push the model onto the stage. The model looked so real, it could easily pass for a live human.

The professor walked to the center of the stage and stood beside the model. His bony hand shook as he reached toward the model's head and uncovered the brain. Next, he opened a hinged door that exposed the lungs, heart, and stomach. The crowd gasped in amazement as they watched the lungs expand and contract. With each heartbeat, vessels carried blood through the body and to the brain.

Professor Virtuoso explained, "This model will perfectly mimic the inner working of the human species. Our team members are going to enter the body and show you how to do the most damage."

The crowd shouted, "Tear it up, that's our job! Tear it up! WOK! WOK! WOK! WOK!"

The professor seemed strengthened by the audience's response. "Let's get started. Cocaine team, come on and help me." From the back of the stage, a rat with a cigarette hanging out of his mouth carried a small amount of cocaine on a serving tray. He carefully placed the tray on the model's knee.

"Now show us how you work," the professor ordered. The powder separated into thousands of tiny specks full of energy and laughter. They acted like the terrorist army but did not wear uniforms.

"We will show you how to destroy a kid," one cocaine terrorist shouted. They all bounced up and down with excitement, eager to perform their dirty work. The drug leaders sat in their golden chairs laughing and enjoying the circus-like atmosphere.

Eyes wide open with anticipation, the professor said, "Go for it, guys. Show them how you work. Enter through the nose." The cocaine particles rushed up the model's shirt and neck, across his face, and into his nose. The audience could see them travel though the blood vessels, some going straight to the heart. With a laser pointer in hand, the professor shakily indicated the heart. The powder cocaine pushed on the heart walls making it beat faster.

"Look at that heart race," he said. "Over time we can badly damage a person's heart. It will beat like this for approximately fifteen minutes to a half hour. We can damage the muscles and main blood vessels to cause heart disease."

The audience watched the cocaine army travel through the blood vessels and explode like fireworks in the brain.

Professor Virtuoso managed to aim his pointer at the brain, "The model now feels great. He is high on drugs and loves the feeling, even though hundreds of his brain cells are being destroyed. Cocaine will change the thinking process of his brain. Give him a half-hour ride and then bring him down."

"Bring him down!" the audience yelled.

The alert model stood up from the chair, full of energy, and moved around the stage. The fireworks in his brain slowed to a dim glow and stopped. Thirty minutes passed as if it were seconds. The professor closed the doors that exposed the brain and other organs.

"The ride's over," Professor Virtuoso explained. "Now he will crash. As great as his high was, his low will be a horrible crash. He will feel sad and depressed and think the only way to feel good again is to get more drugs."

The model's look of pleasure faded. His shoulders slumped, and his knees bent. He crumpled back into the chair.

The professor walked over to the model and asked, "Are you OK?"

"Yes," the model responded, "I'm OK, but I feel really tired and sad."

Professor Virtuoso replied, "More drugs will make you feel better."

"Then give me more," he said. "I want it just one more time."

"This is a training conference, and you are only for training purposes. I had planned on giving you drugs only once."

"I feel awful. Please, help me this one time. Give me one more dose!"

"All right." the professor pointed to the back of the stage and instructed, "Send another team out." From the back of the stage, a rat brought another tray of cocaine and set it on the model's knees. The model sat up, taking notice, and reached for the tray. The professor struck a hard blow to his foot and said, "You only do as you are told."

A brief pause followed before he ordered the cocaine, "Enter his nose."

The terrorists ran up the model's thighs, across his chest, up his neck, and across his face to enter his nose. The model breathed in deeply, sucking them up like a vacuum cleaner. He couldn't get enough of the stuff.

In moments, the model jumped up and danced around. His arms flailed and fingers pointed at no one in particular. He spoke with a fast, exaggerated rhythm that few could understand.

"I'm OK now, everything's fine, good, OK," he shouted. "Thank you! Thank you!"

The powder granules went to his heart, pushing on the walls, causing fast and irregular beats. When the terrorists arrived in his brain, the fireworks lit up again. The model became nervous and jittery. His eyes darted about, his pupils enlarged. He sucked air into his nose to stop mucous from running down his dry lips.

"This is great!" he shouted at the audience while wiping snot from his lip. "I love this stuff! Thanks, man."

Professor Virtuoso scoffed, "He doesn't know it takes only a few times to become addicted. Some humans become addicted the very first time they use."

The model defended himself. "I'm not addicted! I won't use cocaine again because I know how bad it is. I just wanted to try it a second time, that's all."

With a knowing sneer, the professor replied, "Yeah, right."

Turning to the audience, Professor Virtuoso stated, "When we get into a body, the brain loses its ability to have rational thoughts—we gain power over it."

The model, still alert and dancing crazily all over the stage, said, "You don't have power over me. I'm free!"

"We will take you down and make you a slave," the professor replied harshly. "We'll show you how much power you have. You're not free. We own you now."

The militant fanatics shouted, "Take him down! Take him down! He's our slave."

Deceived and in denial, the model said confidently, "I can stop drugs any time I want." The professor stared at the model that was hundreds of times larger than he was, but clueless that he was becoming a cocaine addict.

Again, thirty minutes seemed like thirty seconds to the model. His heart began to beat slower, and the fireworks in his brain stopped, just like before. He stopped dancing and crumpled into the chair.

Professor Virtuoso told him, "Well, your time is up." He motioned to the rats. "Take him out and bring in another model."

The model became frantic. "Wait! Give me one more hit before I leave! Please!"

The professor ordered, "No, that's all. Take him out."

"This is not right!" The model kicked and screamed as the rats pulled him to the back of the stage. "You tricked me. I'll get you, Professor!"

As the rats took the model away, the professor said, "That's right. Tricking you is our job. We'll trick and trap you. You will become an addict, enslaved to cocaine." The crowd laughed and applauded at the sight of the rats dragging the model offstage.

"The first model showed how powerful we are when humans try us just once," the professor bragged. "Bring in the female model!"

The rats brought her to center stage. She was dressed in jeans and a tank top. Heavy makeup covered her face and her upper left arm had a tattoo that read, "I love drugs."

"Bring me a cigarette," Professor Virtuoso ordered.

In obedience, one of the slave-rats did as ordered. He was an addicted servant and hoped his need for drugs would be rewarded later.

"Give it to her," the professor barked at him. The female model took it and placed it between her red lips.

"We're all ultimately going to be sacrificed." Professor Virtuoso excitedly paced back and forth. He was much more energetic than when he came on stage. The crowd wondered if he had snorted a bit of cocaine.

"When you get into a human body, you have one chance, only one chance to accomplish your goal. Are you," he pointed to his audience, "willing to pay the price to hurt innocent children? Are you willing to hurt their parents so they can't take care of their own kids? Are you willing to destroy the entire human species?"

The crowd shouted in frenzied unison, pumping their fists up and down, "We are willing! We will destroy them!"

Mr. Flatulent joined the professor, "Tobacco group, stand to your feet." All over the arena, tobacco terrorists stood up, feeling giddy to be singled out.

"You," he shouted, "are on the front line. Most kids start with you or marijuana. That should make you proud enough to work even harder. Your addictive drug, nicotine, is where many kids begin their path to addiction. When they start out with you, they are making a statement: 'I am my own person, old enough and mature enough to make my own decisions.' In the beginning, you make them dizzy and sometimes they even get sick, but that doesn't stop them. They want to be independent from parents and caregivers, so they continue to make their statement by smoking. I want you to know that you have a reason to be proud of yourselves. You look so innocent, yet cause so much harm."

"Let's talk to our friends," the professor said. He looked at the end of the cigarette and spoke to the tobacco particles. "Come out and talk to us." Some of the tobacco pieces climbed out of the end of the cigarette and stood on top of it.

"Tell us how you do your job," the professor instructed.

One of the particles stepped forward and said, "We go straight to the brain and massage it to make humans feel relaxed. That makes them ignore the damage we do to their bodies."

Another stepped forward and added, "We go to the heart and eventually cause heart disease."

"We attack soft, pink lungs to make them brown and stiff. We cause cancer and emphysema. Together," they locked arms, "we are killers."

"What other purpose do you serve?" the professor asked.

"None. Our only goal is to hurt people. Bodies are not designed to breathe smoke. It amazes me that the human species will put things in their bodies with no concern about the damage. They make decisions without thinking. They turn terrorists loose in their bodies and that is so-o-o stupid."

The professor turned to the audience, "Little kids are smart and haven't developed many bad habits, so we have to trick them. While part of our team goes to their brains to make them feel relaxed, others destroy their bodies." Pointing to the cigarette, he said, "I'm going to light you up, and you can show us how you work together."

The particles eagerly ran off the top of the paper and back into the end of the cigarette. Once they were back in their places, shouts erupted from inside the cigarette, "Light us up! We're ready."

The professor instructed the rat to strike a match and light the cigarette. As smoke curled upward, the model inhaled, pulling smoke deep into her lungs.

Virtuoso said excitedly, "Watch this!" He opened the door to the model's chest cavity so the heart and lungs were exposed. Using his laser pointer, he indicated the lungs.

"When you get into human lungs, they are disgustingly clean and pink, like a newborn baby's skin. I hate the sight of clean lungs. When the job of tobacco is done, these lungs won't be pink any longer. I love to see dirty, brown lungs."

The professor's eyes glistened with anticipation. "Some of you will go to the walls of the lungs to hang around for years, crawling in and out of the pores and crevices. That will be your job. As the human continues to smoke, your friends and coworkers will join your efforts on the lung walls. The lungs will darken as you travel through the bronchial tubes to the lungs. Hang on to those walls, and do some extensive damage!

"Over time many of these once-healthy specimens will develop breathing problems and bronchial infections. We are ruining their ability to breathe. The more they smoke, the quicker those pink lungs turn black. We love black lungs! Hopefully cancer will eat its way in and eventually kill them."

The professor was pumped with excitement, despite his obvious physical limitations. The terrorists had never met anyone so enthusiastic about their mission. They roared with laughter as he mocked the model.

With an evil cackle, Professor Virtuoso continued. "You are not limited to cancer. You're free to do all kinds of damage." Pointing to the heart, he continued. "Some of you will flow through the bloodstream straight toward the heart. Your presence restricts blood flow, which leads to heart and vessel damage. Now the stupid human is set up for heart trouble. I love my job!" he added.

The crowd shouted, "WOK! WOK! Nothing will stop us now!"

"You would think," the professor eagerly went on, "that when humans learn this, they would choose not to smoke. But the process is so slow they think it will never affect them. For some of you it is smooth sailing to the brain." He dragged out "smoo-o-o-th" and attempted to indicate smoothness with his hand, but he was shaking too much. Nothing about his body was in smooth working order anymore. He opened the model's head to expose the brain.

"Tell us what you're doing," he said to the terrorists in the brain.

"We are making her relax, relieving her tension. She loves that calm feeling. We'll do this for fifteen or twenty minutes, then stop and just disappear."

"Do you want me to tell you what happens next?" Professor Virtuoso asked the audience.

"When she gets a little tense, she will remember how we made her relax. She will want another smoke." The tobacco terrorists continued to massage her brain and damage her heart and lungs. Suddenly, they all vanished.

Professor Virtuoso was so motivated that he stepped off the platform and paced the aisles. "You," he pointed to individual terrorists, "have the privilege to ravage young bodies!" He proclaimed his message of bondage for kids who will say yes to cigarettes.

"Years later we can watch their bodies wither away. Very few kids are mature enough to think for themselves. If they could talk with their parents about their struggles, maybe they would have the courage to say no. Maybe they would say, 'Not me! I won't be tricked!' But parents are generally too busy or unconcerned to listen. Kids smoke to fit in with their peers and relieve the tension they are feeling. Instead of turning to their parents, they turn to you. Oh, the beauty of addiction!"

The terrorists joined the professor's enthusiasm and shouted, "Hoorah! Hoorah! We have them! Now, they are ours to destroy. WOK! WOK!"

"So here's the real deal," Professor Virtuoso said. "Let's make a deal with the smart kids who make stupid decisions."

He spoke mockingly now, as though to a kid. "We will make you look really cool and help you relax. Along with that gift we will give you breathing problems, heart and lung problems, and most likely, cancer. Sounds to me like a great deal for a kid."

"You're are right, Professor, it's a great deal!" Mr. Flatulent laughed. "Now everyone give your best cheer of thanks to Professor Virtuoso for his exciting presentation!"

The crowd clapped, whistled and stomped their feet as the professor bowed and made his slow exit from the stage.

# Humans Make Their Appearance at the "War on Kids" Conference

Mr. Flatulent addressed the crowd, "I want you to focus your attention now on our reporters in the 'hood."

Big C and Mari Jane, cocaine and marijuana terrorists, appeared on the screen. They were perched on top of a mailbox in front of a pawn shop. Their camera operator filmed a continuous stream of people walking in and out of the pawnshop carrying computers, jewelry, construction tools, bicycles, and other items. On both sides of the street were tall apartment buildings with kids playing on the sidewalks. Tiny, grassless yards were littered with trash. The buildings had a market, music store, used clothing store, bar, and liquor store. Graffiti and gang signs plastered the brick walls. The camera focused on the door of the pawnshop, but occasionally scanned the streets showing a population of young and old humans of various races.

Big C described the activity. "Many of these people are selling what they own or what they stole, to get drugs. Look at them. We own them! They will do anything for drugs. We are the most important thing in their lives."

The camera scanned the street as a car slowed. It pulled to a stop at the curb in front of a rundown, four-story apartment complex. Half a block away a group of five or six teenagers were hanging out and signaling at cars as they passed. All of them wore jeans and gray T-shirts. When the small group of teens spotted a police cruiser moving slowly down the street, they scattered in different directions between the buildings. When the cops were gone, they emerged just as suddenly, back to their place on the sidewalk.

Mari Jane began, "Those young humans work for us. 'Street pharmacists' is what we call them—drug dealers. Their addicted customers call a cell phone number and place their orders. The dealer tells them when to come for the pick-up."

As she was speaking, an old car pulled up to the curb where the boys were standing. One of them looked in all directions before stepping to the passenger side. A thin, pale woman lowered the window and extended her closed hand. In one quick motion, the boy took money from her hand, replaced it with drugs, and the car drove away.

Mari Jane said, "You have just watched a drug deal go down. It only takes a few seconds. The dealers are high school dropouts with little supervision. They think selling drugs is the only way they can survive. They will live in the streets, become addicts, or be in and out of prison most of their lives."

A handsome, black businessman stopped his new luxury car. The same hand-to-hand exchange took place, and the silver car sped away.

"Rich and poor come down here. That man will lose his fancy car soon."

A tall, thin white man approached one of the young boys on the sidewalk. After a few words, the boy walked into a narrow opening between the buildings. Minutes later, he returned to the man, who waited nervously on the sidewalk. After they made an exchange, the man crossed the street and entered an old, dilapidated apartment building.

"That's one of my favorite places," Big C said, pointing to the apartment building. "It's a crack house, a place where addicts go to use drugs. There is normally a dealer inside. Let me show you around."

Big C, Mari Jane, and the camera operator scurried down the mailbox and a drainpipe to the sidewalk. They dodged in and out of traffic to get to the other side of the street, headed for the entrance to a building with the windows boarded up. As someone opened the door, sunlight revealed a scrawny, glassy-eyed woman. Her greasy, dirty hair barely covered an injury on the side of her face. Her blouse hung off one shoulder, and her skirt was torn. She moved slowly, like someone in a trance.

A man sitting on the scummy floor at the end of the dark hall yelled, "Get out of here, you filthy tramp, and don't come back! Go home and take care of our kids."

Big C looked into the camera and said excitedly, "This is fantastic! She's spending her money on us while her kids are at home alone."

The only light in the dirty building filtered through the cracks between the boards on the windows and the open doors. Men and women of various races and ages were sitting around the dim, smoke-hazed rooms. Trash, clothes, broken crack pipes, and old needles were scattered over the floor. It smelled of urine and foul odors that were unrecognizable.

Big C exclaimed, "It doesn't get any better than this, man! Look at all the humans wrecking their lives. This is not the only crack house in the city. Sometimes the police will make a drug bust and board up the building, but the addicts and dealers just move to another location.

"Well, that's it from the hood. The things you have seen here today are the norm—nothing unusual. Hey, all you conference terrorists, listen up. Every human has a conscience, a sense of right and wrong. It's a disadvantage for the drug dealers, but drugs will numb the human conscience. After that, humans don't care who they hurt. If you can get kids to use drugs, they might quit school, become adults who can't keep jobs, and end up in a lovely place like this. Now, back to you at WOK headquarters."

# Rappers

Mr. Flatulent took center stage. "We have an interview set up with the popular rap group, Irresponsibility. They can't see us, but they can hear us with their ear buds. Give a big cheer of welcome to Irresponsibility."

The screen lit up, and the faces of four young men appeared. The camera scanned down to show their baggy, mid-calf pants. The crotches of their pants sagged down to their knees, leaving colorful designer boxers exposed. Two of the rappers were bald, with tattoos of marijuana leaves on their heads. One had dreadlocks and the other a long, braided ponytail. Their shirts had phrases that read "DRUGS RULE" and "DOWN WITH AUTHORITY." Shouts and applause drowned out every other sound as the crowd of terrorists welcomed them. Their enthusiasm excited Irresponsibility. When the crowd finally settled down, Mr. Flatulent began his interview.

"Thank you for taking time out of your busy day for our conference. You are one of the hottest human groups in the world, but some adults are critical of your music. For instance, I'm holding an article from the *Notaware Times* that states, 'Some rappers and some of their music are influencing our kids in the wrong way.' What do you have to say about that?"

The leader of the group, who called himself Rebel, flipped his dreadlocks over his shoulder and said, "We rap about what we believe and how we live. If they don't like it, it's their problem. Free country, free speech."

Flatulent asked, "Do you feel you have any responsibility to young humans?"

"No, I am not responsible for anyone but myself. When I was a kid, no one was responsible for me. I raised myself and made my own decisions. The kids that like our music can decide for themselves. We are just entertainers."

"You are exactly right," Mr. Flatulent agreed. "We feel the same way. I have another article by a well-known politician and religious leader who said, 'The group Irresponsibility is causing many young people to experiment with drugs and alcohol. Some of those kids have become addicts, and a few overdosed and died. The band not only promotes chemical abuse in their music, but they also use drugs. I know because they have been arrested for drug possession.' Do you have any comment?"

One of the bald rappers, Coward, stepped forward with an angry expression on his face.

"Yeah, I got a comment. We have a job to do, same as you. We don't care what those old fogies say. Our job is to make music. What's your job, dude?" he asked Mr. Flatulent.

"You know me well enough. I am a drug. My job is to turn humans into drug addicts."

"See what I mean," said Coward. "My job is to make music. Parents and religious freaks can't make me stop. Who are adults to tell kids what to do?" He thrust his finger forcefully toward the camera. "If lamebrain kids get addicted, what do we care? They're just a bunch of stupid, idiot kids."

"Why do they call you Coward?" Mr. Flatulent asked.

"I feel scared and insecure when I'm sober, but when I use drugs, I feel brave," Coward responded.

"You guys are a part of our family," Mr. Flatulent responded. "We thank you, Irresponsibility, for being a group of rebels. You speak for us with your words and actions. You are like heroes to thousands of kids, influencing them to use drugs and alcohol. Everyone here is proud of your musical lies that promote the work of our humans in the streets! Thanks for your assistance. Keep up the good work."

Addressing the audience, he added, "Okay, family members, show your appreciation." Again, the drug terrorists erupted in roaring applause. Mr. Flatulent turned to the camera and said, "Let's go to our next location."

# Stardust and Diamond

A pretty, twenty-five year-old blond woman filled the screen. Cosmetics enhanced her large eyes, high cheekbones, and full, round lips. She was dressed in tight-fitting white pants and a pink tank top that revealed too much and left little to the imagination. A sparkling designer handbag hung from her shoulder. In the background, a group of teenagers, obviously thrilled to see the very popular rock star, waved their hands and screamed, “Stardust, we love you!” Others just yelled her name repeatedly, “Stardust! Stardust! Stardust!”

A roped-off area kept them a safe distance away, and security guards watched from close by. Stardust’s business manager, who called himself Diamond, was a middle-aged man dressed in a shiny suit and tie. His black hair and gray beard were perfectly groomed. A careful inspection could not have found one hair out of place. Walking next to Stardust, he stayed with her like a shadow.

"I want to thank you," Mr. Flatulent said, "for giving a few minutes to our annual War on Kids Conference."

Flashing brilliant white teeth, Stardust purred, "You are so welcome. You are my friends."

"Yes," replied Flatulent, "and you are a great friend of ours, promoting our continued success. The media has portrayed you as 'the bad girl of entertainment.' Some of your fans' parents are outraged about the way you dress, and they claim your suggestive dance moves are a bad example. Your pictures have recently been on TV and in all the papers. One of them showed you handcuffed and getting into a police car after an arrest for public intoxication. You've had two charges for driving under the influence within the last year. Is there a possibility you might be doing some serious jail time? What do you have to say about all this?"

Stardust replied in a bored tone, "Yeah, the judge wants me to go to rehab. That is so totally lame. I do not have a problem! I'm not a bad person. I just like to party." She swung her hip to the side and raised her arms in a signature dance move. "Besides that, the drugs they found in my car were not mine."

Diamond stepped forward. "Let me say something for her. She is going to rehab so she can become a good example for young girls. Stardust knows what she did was wrong and said she will never do it again. That's the end of this interview."

Mr. Flatulent said, "Thanks for your time."

Stardust and Diamond turned so she could wave at her screaming fans. As she walked away, she spoke defiantly to her manager, but loud enough for all to hear, "I didn't do anything wrong, and I'm not going to that stupid rehab! I will dress any way I like and party whenever I want. The only example I plan to be is how to party and get high."

The camera focused on her handbag. A crack cocaine terrorist slipped out of the top of the bag waving, yelling, and laughing at the camera. "We're still here, and she wants us to go with her to rehab! What a great ride!"

As Diamond opened the limousine door for her, he replied, "I don't care what parents think, Stardust baby, but we have to keep that a secret from the public so we can make a lot of money." The crowd at the conference waved and laughed as the screen went blank.

# Hershel Hash, Attorney at Law

In a rush, Mr. Flatulent instructed the control booth, "Don't waste time. Quickly take us to the next interview with one of my favorite human groups. They are helping to legalize marijuana for social and medical use. Gotta love that! We don't know what human medical experts might decide, but the truth is, some humans just want to smoke a little dope. They will use their medical problems to excuse smoking weed."

A mixed-culture group of twenty or thirty adults appeared on the screen. Some of the men and women wore business suits, but most were casually dressed. Several in the crowd wore tattered shirts, shorts, or dirty jeans. It was a diverse group of well-educated individuals and high school dropouts.

They listened to an expressive speaker who was obviously well educated, but his expensive suit hung loosely on his thin body. He was unshaved and looked like he just got out of bed.

"My name is Hershel Hash," the speaker began. "I am an attorney and former government official. I lead the effort to convince government officials and the general population that marijuana is not addictive and will have no negative effects on users. It should be legalized everywhere, just like alcohol. It will take time, but it's a matter of freedom of choice." He paused for applause. "We are gaining momentum. It has already been approved for medical use in some regions and for social use in others. We have convinced a large percentage of the population that it has no negative effects. It won't be long before it's legalized for social use throughout the country.

"We have opponents, but we have good friends operating in secret on our behalf. We can't see them right now, but our audio unit is set up to hear them. They are having their annual get-together and want to interview me about our future expansion."

The voice of Mr. Flatulent asked, "Can you hear me? Do we have sound?"

Attorney Hash answered, "Yes, we can hear you. How is your conference going?"

Flatulent answered, "Intense! Let me ask you, how is your progress in getting the government to legalize marijuana for social use?"

"It's slow. There's a lot of opposition. Counselors, psychiatrists, research centers, and religious nuts are trying to stop us."

"Mr. Hash, here's some of the resistance you're going to get. Educators say a stoned kid cannot learn as well and will have abnormal social development. University medical centers say they have proof that smoking marijuana a couple of time a week can damage the brain. They say damage is serious in kids and those under age twenty-five, because the brain is still developing. Law officials think marijuana use will cause more driving accidents. Counselors believe that legalizing marijuana for social use is a bad decision, because it will become easily accessible to kids and hurt more families. Experts say that kids who start with marijuana will try other dangerous drugs." Mr. Flatulent continued, "How will you deal with all that?"

"I don't represent the truth or the consequences of drug use. We are in it for the money. I represent my clients, which means I must ignore some of the truth. I must present a façade, a false image, to block people from hearing the true effects. If the public gets too many hints about how I really operate, it will slow our progress."

"You're my kind of attorney!" Flatulent said proudly. "Like me, you don't have a conscience, so it's easy to ignore the truth. I have just a few more questions. Rehab centers have kids and adults trying to kick the habit, especially teens and school drop-outs. How do you respond to that?"

"We ignore it. That's their problem!"

"Does marijuana help you with a medical condition?"

"I don't have a medical condition, but my doctor thinks I do."

"How much do you smoke, Mr. Hash?"

"Every chance I get," he responded with a snicker.

Flatulent encouraged Attorney Hash. "Keep up the good work and thanks for your time."

"You're welcome. Good luck."

# "We Don't Care" Tobacco

"We have more special guests today." Mr. Flatulent introduced a new video where eight men, all wearing stylish suits and silk ties, sat at a large executive table surrounded by walls covered with advertisements for WDC cigarettes. One of the perfectly dressed men was in a wheelchair, and another breathed with the help of an oxygen tank. Their fancy clothes could not conceal their unhealthy appearance.

Mr. Flatulent motioned to the conference guests. "Please welcome our partners in purpose, the board of directors of the WDC Tobacco Company and their honorable president, Mr. Greed. It fills me with pride that this human company shares our motto: We Don't Care." Mr. Greed, a handsome specimen of good health, rose from the table and stepped forward.

The crowd applauded and shouted their greeting, "WOK! WOK! WOK! We don't care."

Flatulent turned to Mr. Greed and said, "This is our greatest conference ever. We are excited to hear your words of encouragement."

Mr. Greed smiled into the camera. "What an honor this is for me, my board of directors, and all the members of the Greed family to join you today. Thank you for working hard to achieve our common goals. United we stand! If you fail, we all fail; and if we at WDC fail, I will have to get a real job." The crowd roared with laughter.

Mr. Flatulent asked a daring question: "Mr. Greed, could I ask, uh, do you smoke?" The audience went silent. Every eye turned to Mr. Greed. *Did he smoke?*

Mr. Greed sternly answered, "Are you kidding? That would be stupid." Pointing toward the vice president, he continued. "Look, he can barely breathe. He started smoking when he was only twelve, because he thought it was so cool. And look closely at the rest of these guys. They all started when they were just boys. Now they can't do much because they have health problems caused from smoking." He ended with a laugh. "They smell bad and have stinky breath, but they have a lot of money."

Flatulent asked, "What do you say to your children about smoking?"

Mr. Greed answered soberly, "My kids are a different story. I love them and tell them they are too smart to smoke. I tell them they should not start this disgusting habit. Not my kids."

Flatulent wondered aloud, "Then what steps will ensure the expansion of our purpose?"

"Kids can't see how harmful it is, so they want to try it. The secret is to trick them when they're young. The younger, the better, because once they become addicted, it's so hard for them to stop. They will smoke for years and have to pay us for every pack of cigarettes. People never start smoking because they want to be addicted or because they like smoking. They start because they want to fit in and try something new. They just want to look cool.

"Never forget, we are WDC—We Don't Care. We will continue manufacturing cigarettes because people become addicted. We don't put guns to their heads! We just influence them so they will want to smoke. Let 'em light up!"

Mr. Flatulent topped it off with, "We are not like humans. We feel no guilt and have no morals. Our one and only purpose is to hurt people."

Encouraging the crowd, he said, "Let's show our appreciation for the humans who are willing to deceive people, take their money, cause diseases, and feel no shame about doing it. They are our partners in destruction—just like us—no guilt!" In honor of the humans, the terrorists responded with dancing and screams of, "We Don't Care!"

# The End of Halfweed

The conference was in full swing, the crowd busy with activities. A guard walked through the crowd, unnoticed, toward the control booth. He had worked many conferences. He knew the lead camera operator who was quiet and shy, unlike the particle that had pushed past the registration desk. The different-looking camera and the way the crew had entered the building made him suspicious.

He stopped a short distance from Halfweed and stared at her until he was convinced that an imposter was operating the camera. Remembering the female prisoner, he left the conference and jogged to the holding cell. He hid close enough to see the guards, but careful to stay out of sight. It was clear to him that the guards were imposters. He cautiously retreated to the conference center and assembled twenty-five or thirty guards to march with him to the cell.

The Nopers who were posing as guards saw them coming and

realized they were going to be overthrown. Uncertain what to do, they huddled together and made a quick decision to run for safety. They reasoned that they could be of no value if destroyed. But if they could hide from the terrorists, they might survive and be able to continue in the fight. They escaped just in time.

The conference guards untied the two terrorist camera operators and listened to their story of capture by Halfweed and her group of traitors. They also told the guards that Halfweed was using a camera that was remotely controlled by a human who was watching the conference.

The angry camera crew was restrained from barging into the conference. The conference leaders would not want the embarrassment of such an interruption. Instead, a guard delivered a note to Hack explaining the situation.

Seated with the other leaders in their golden chairs, Hack opened the note and read it. His facial expression changed from smiling, proud leader to furious. Halfweed had embarrassed him once, and he would not let it happen again. His mind raced, searching for a way to destroy her without leaving his place of honor among the other leaders. Hack motioned for the research team and whispered something to them. He told them to get the name of the human who was watching the conference and to get the gang leaders and drug dealers on camera.

The conference was ending with the terrorists getting their assignments and motivational speeches to go out and destroy lives. As the final speaker took the microphone, Hack rose from his chair of honor, walked to center stage, and asked for the microphone.

"This has been a great conference!" After the applause stopped, he continued, "But one of our own family has betrayed us." Everyone gasped, and the room became instantly quiet.

Halfweed looked at her fellow Nopers who had stayed close and followed instructions to help her. She said to them, "We have a problem. I want you to stand tall and appear strong, even if you don't feel strong. Do not let them scare you!"

The angry voice of Hack crackled through the sound system. "I have been informed that a human has been. . . and is . . . as I speak . . . watching us."

Mouths fell open in shock, and faces froze in the silence. They were confused and not sure what to do. How could a human be watching when the conference was safely hidden in the slime pit of the world?

Hack's bony finger pointed toward Halfweed. "The one who double-crossed us is at the camera with a few of her followers. Her name is Halfweed, and her followers call themselves the Nopers. Grab them and bring them down front!"

Like swarms of bees, the terrorists surrounded Halfweed and her Nopers. They tore off their headbands and pushed them forward toward Hack. The conference crew regained control of the camera.

The furious crowd booed and shouted, "Traitors! We hate you as much as we hate kids! We will destroy you."

Hack glared into the camera. "To the human watching by camera I say, you will be sorry for intruding into our underworld. We serve the heartless humans who sell drugs and don't care who they destroy. You can watch as we throw Halfweed and her friends into the water! They will dissolve and disappear into the great sewer in the ground. Ha!" Hack's body shook with laughter and coughing while the other leaders high-fived each other in relief that the Nopers were caught.

Hack turned to the terrorist leaders. "Would any of you like to say anything to the disgusting human watching us?" They all jumped to their feet and headed toward center stage. They had never had an argument among themselves because their goals were the same: destroy the future of the human species. But this was different. They felt their power over young minds was threatened. They pushed and shoved each other to be the first to speak.

Hack jabbed a finger toward the camera and said, "Hey, you—parents, step-parents, and caregivers! I am coming after your kids! Do you want to know what we do? We can show you our tricks, and we will still trap your kids."

# Crack Speaks to Humans

Hack extended his hand in a gesture of welcome to his friend. Crack stepped up to the platform. His evil eyes gazed into the camera. He hated kids and destroying them made him very happy.

Crack's frightening voice began, saying "They call me Crack, Ready Rock, or Gravel. I have a job to do, and that job is to trick kids. The easiest kids to trick are in homes where there is lots of arguing, not much fun, and almost no supervision. I look for kids who are being hurt by offensive words that are used like whips to damage their emotions. Words are the most powerful weapon available to your species. Words have the power to build up or tear down, to encourage or discourage. Words cause kids to move forward to success or give up and become quitters. Kids who are being criticized and told they are stupid make my job simple!"

Crack motioned to the camera crew. "Show the clip of the little girl getting beat up with hurtful words!" he shouted. "Our research team made an animated video of the power of words. Words can be like a lion tamer snapping a whip. Look at that tongue popping out hurtful words! Every snap hits the little girl's mind to create painful, emotional scars.

"Many humans don't understand the damage that can be caused by cruel words. Some adults think that calling kids bad names will make them want to behave better. But kids who are abused with words become easy targets for us. They are confused and angry and want to feel better about themselves. That's where I come in to trick them!"

"Hey! Are there any kids out there listening? I'm coming after you! When you try me you'll think I can take away the pain caused by the hurtful words. You'll believe I can end your feelings of rejection and sadness. All I need to do is wait until the right time and BAM! I gotcha!"

"Hey kids, I'm coming after you!"

# Personal Invitation to Prison

While Crack was speaking, Prescription Drugs changed out of his terrorist uniform. At Hack's prompting, he strutted to center stage dressed to mock humans. A big, gold chain dangled around his neck, and his cap was turned sideways.

"Who are you?" Prescription Drugs spoke to the camera with an undertone of rage. "Are you a computer nerd kid that broke through our security system? Are you mad because you can't get all the stuff you want?" He hopped around waving his arms and pointing with sharp jabs into the camera. "Maybe your family and neighbors are all mad and angry for the same reason.

"Are some of your family members drug addicts? If you want to grow up and be like them, I'm the man to help you." His hands waved through the air. "Start using drugs when you're young! You'll have a lot of fun, then an entire life of misery." The audience

cheered him on with screams of approval.

"You think you're not special because your family has no time for you. Maybe you're alone a lot because they work so much. I betcha I know something about you that you don't even know. You are a special, important creation, but no one tells you that, do they? You think the 'hood will be your future.

"You don't realize that the family you were born into doesn't have to determine your future. You can quit school, start stealing, join a gang, hang out, and start smoking dope. Yeah, you can join our team, be a drug dealer, and ruin lives. We will help you get out of the 'hood so you won't have to live in that scary place. Let me show you one of our success stories. His crib is spic and span—no dirt there, man!"

He pointed to the screen. "Meet 121 ADIH, one of our success stories. We helped him get out of the 'hood to the big house. Check out the big tattoo on his neck. He's a gang banger. 121 ADIH, show us what you got when you joined our team and got out of your bad neighborhood."

121 ADIH began a tour of his house, speaking as if he were a real estate agent trying to impress a buyer. "Hey, bro, you wanna come live wit' me?" 121 ADIH was standing in a concrete court-yard surrounded by large buildings with bars on the windows. There were big towers with guards holding large, automatic weapons. A very high fence enclosed everything you could see. Hundreds of men stood around, some in small groups and others alone, but all wore the same color clothes.

The terrorist leader, Prescription Drugs, added, "See all those men? Most of them are our friends."

121 ADIH entered a building and walked down a long hallway, past rows of small cells with doors made of iron bars. He stopped at one of them and said, "This is my crib. I got a bed, a few books, a sink, and a toilet. Real nice, huh? I got a roommate so I ain't never alone. I never think about what time to go to bed or get up. I have a schedule that tells me what to do, where to go, what to wear, and what to eat. You don't worry about nuttin' at my house."

121 ADIH walked back out to the big yard. "If you wanna go no-where in life, you can live in the Big House too. Hope to see you soon."

"Thanks, 121 ADIH," said Prescription Drugs. "He was a smart kid, but he thought it was cool to quit school and hang out with the other quitters. His parents weren't around much so the gang became his family. He chose to become a criminal and now he gets to live in that prison for the next ten years. I congratulate him for his great failure!"

Prescription Drugs glared into the camera and finished with a loud, harsh voice saying, "We are coming after you—you little know-it-all kid! Quit school, start stealing, get a job you hate, and be angry because you're poor. Use some drugs to feel good. Sell some drugs to get money for more drugs, and eventually you can go live with 121 ADIH."

121 ADIH

# Trapped Behind a Mask

Another terrorist named Weed came to the stage. With every word he spoke there was a small puff of smoke.

"Most of you will be tricked long before your teenage years, but you won't know it. We know you listen to people who don't really care about you. You spend time looking in a mirror wondering what needs to be changed. You think, *Am I too tall or too short? Am I too skinny or too big? Are my eyes too small? Is my nose too big?* On and on you go, not liking yourself and rejecting who you are.

"When you reject who you are, you try to make up for it by copying others. Some of you are told you are not smart enough to succeed. You think you were born into the wrong family or nationality. Eventually, you will become a bad copy of someone else and lose sight of how unique you really are. When we trick you, the person you really are becomes trapped behind a mask of public image.

"Television and music videos tell you what to wear and how to

look so you will be accepted. You will try to remake your appearance, intellect, and abilities to fit the images. You'll do anything to get approval from others.

"In time, you won't know who you are because you have become a fake. You will reject who you really are and pretend to be someone else. You'll feel sad and lonely, and that's when you'll start liking drugs. We will make you feel good, at least for a little while.

You don't want others to laugh at you so you'll smoke me, Weed, to fit in. After all, I look so innocent!"

"Shut up! You're telling them too much." The audience booed, stamped their feet, and shouted at the speaker. "Sit down and be quiet. You've said enough."

Hack pranced up to Weed. "Good job. You told humans the truth about themselves. No problem, we can still trick them." Hack quiet-ed the terrorists and said, "Don't worry. Kids are non-thinkers. They will still get caught in our trap."

# Alcohol Enticement

Brew and Stumble staggered to the stage. One swayed back and forth while the other nearly fell down. Everyone laughed at their display of drunkenness.

"Hey kid! Is that a kid out there watching us?" Stumble almost fell down. "My job is to convince you to try alcohol while you are young. When you put me in your body you will feel good, but you might do something stupid, possibly dangerous. I will give you a false feeling of confidence. You won't be shy when you drink me. I will numb your conscience so you will do things that you know are wrong, but you won't feel any guilt until later. Your brain will not function normally, and you won't think clearly. You might become angry and try to hurt your family or friends. The younger you start drinking alcohol, the greater chance you have of becoming an alcoholic."

Stumble's slurred voice rose expressively. "Some of you will die in car wrecks. I love that! And others will wreck their own lives."

Brew looked into the camera. "Beer advertisements make you believe you need it to have a good time at parties, sporting events and family gatherings. They never show you the bad picture of families that are destroyed because of alcoholism, car wrecks, and sickness.

"I have no conscience so I don't care who I hurt. I will soak your brain so you can escape to a fantasy world for a short time. You will say to yourself, 'Everyone is doing it. It's normal to drink and get drunk. It's just a part of life. How can it be bad?'

"Many adult alcoholics were just little kids when I tricked them!" He pointed to the camera as though he knew a kid was watching. "Remember, I have no conscience so I feel no guilt about hurting you. Drinking alcohol is risky and can be dangerous, but you are blind to my traps. My name is Brew, and I'm waiting to trick you!"

# Mob of Terrorists

Hack motioned for the remaining drug leaders to join him in the spotlight so they could speak to the humans. Sniff, a drug from the family of inhalants, walked forward with a beautiful, smiling female on each arm. His voice sounded hollow, like he was in a barrel.

"You want to sniff some fumes?" He grinned and flashed his big gold tooth. "My family lives in paint, grease removers, and dissolvents, but what I really like to do is dissolve your brain! If you huff me I will make you clumsy, give you really bad headaches, and damage your memory. In school you will be able to answer questions with a brilliant 'duh . . . huh.'" He paused and looked puzzled, "I had something to say but forgot it." Laughter, whistles, and shouts of approval echoed through the pipes.

"Who are your pretty friends? What drug family do they come from?"

"They represent the newest drug on the streets— they don't even have a name yet. They disguise themselves in glamorous clothes and big smiles to hide how dangerous they really are. They trick humans by making the drug world appear exciting. Kids like new adventures and become curious about experimenting with such a good feeling."

"Do you ladies have a message for humans?" Hack extended the microphone to them.

The two responded like a duet. Their soft voices gently stroked the ears of the audience. "Do you want to be beautiful and happy like we are? Do you want attention from boys? Forget the idea that inward beauty is more important than outward beauty. We can show you how to dress like a movie star, be flirty, look a little trashy and get attention. If you use drugs or alcohol with the guys, one of them will treat you like his girlfriend. You can forget your morals do whatever your boyfriend wants and eventually get a great guy just like Sniff!"

A pile of white powder seemed to float forward. Looking closely you could see each granule was a slithering snake with hollow, dead eyes. Hundreds of them entwined, curling around each other, moving like one living thing. One of the larger granules began to speak. "They call us Coke, Snow, Blow, and Nose Candy. Look at us, kid!" he shouted. "You little wimp! We have a gift for you. We will give you the most thrilling sensation you can imagine, like floating on a cloud for about twenty or thirty minutes." Each granule lowered its frightening head like a ballerina bowing after a dance.

"There are a few things we will guarantee. Addiction works the same for everyone. We will take away your self-control, your health and common sense. You will give us your money, your morals, and your future, and become a miserable, rude person. Your family will avoid you. We can become your best friends, and eventually, we will be your only friends. Guaranteed!"

Standing next to Hack was an old soldier of the powerful heroin forces. He interrupted, "Hey, I'm Smack. You kids never start with me, but you graduate to the privilege of using me. A little nicotine, a little alcohol, plus a little cocaine, and before you know it, you are injecting me into your veins. I can help you get AIDS and hepatitis, which can make you very sick and kill you. Come on down to the bottom. I'll be waiting for you. I can take you as low as you want to go."

# Archives

"Let's go to the old videos and show some of our success stories." Hack directed the camera operator. He waved for Opiate to come forward. "She's a strong warrior whose cousin is named Prescription Drugs. Tell us about this video."

Opiate walked to the microphone as Slur followed close behind. Slur belched, farted, and vomited on the floor, but did not go around the stinking mess. He walked straight through the gooey puddle, leaving sticky tracks on the floor!

Opiate laughed at Slur and told the crowd, "When you drink a lot, you can be rude, crude, and not care what others think. Drink more alcohol and make a fool of yourself, just like Slur!"

She pointed to the jumbo screen, "That girl is six-year-old

Mary." In the home video, a pretty little girl with silky black hair made goofy faces as she skipped toward the camera. Her smile lit up the screen, and family members laughed at her silliness. Opiate told the camera crew to bring up the next video.

"This," Opiate pointed, "is Mary at sixteen. She is sitting in her first car." The crowd of terrorists watched the young, black-haired beauty enjoying life in the shiny red sports car. The video changed unexpectedly to a photo of the red car with the front-end crushed into the side of another car. The driver was slumped over the steering wheel with bloody gashes on her head and face. A police officer peered through the car's shattered windshield.

"This was Mary when she was eighteen," Opiate said, smiling. "Mary liked to take pills, drink, and drive. I think she was exceptionally pretty in this picture."

The video cut to scenes of a funeral. Friends and family members sobbed as they hugged each other at Mary's graveside. The camera zoomed to the top of Mary's casket where Alcohol and Opiate terrorists laughed, danced, and joked about taking another young life. They enjoyed watching Mary's family suffer. The humans could not see the terrorists, but there they were, celebrating their latest accomplishment.

Opiate's voice was quiet and charming. "This is one of my favorite scenes. All of those people at the cemetery loved Mary. They will certainly miss her, but her death doesn't bother me. I give these kids the pleasure they crave, then I kill them. Oh, by the way, let me introduce myself; they call me Opiate. I am available at the pharmacy, on the streets, and maybe in the adults' medicine stashes." She bent her knees and lowered her body forward in a graceful curtsy. The devious forces were dazzled by her presentation.

A school picture of a young boy appeared, and Hack continued. "Spineless, come tell us this boy's story. My friend Spineless is in the Meth family. He's one of the quickest at turning humans into addicts and making them useless."

Spineless looked at the screen. "This seven-year old cutie is David."

Another picture appeared. "Now, here he is at fifteen." David was walking down the street holding hands with a girl about the same age. They seemed to be enjoying themselves, laughing and talking. David's free hand held a cigarette.

"David started to smoke at the age of twelve," Spineless said proudly. "Bring up the next picture."

There was David with Casey, his girlfriend, holding a newborn baby. Casey rested in her hospital bed looking carefree and happy. David held the baby up to the home video camera, grinning from ear to ear, and said, "This is my son, David, Jr. Isn't he a cute little guy?" He held his son even closer so the camera could get a better shot of the two-day-old infant.

Another video showed David in a courtroom, standing with an attorney in front of a judge. Casey and David's four-year-old namesake sat on the front row listening to the judge speak directly to David.

"You were warned many times to quit using and selling drugs, but you chose to continue. You have become a common criminal to support your drug habit. I hereby sentence you to five years in prison." To declare his decision final, the judge stood up to walk to his chambers while saying loudly, "Court dismissed."

"Wait! I will quit, Your Honor. I promise," yelled David.

An officer of the court handcuffed David and escorted him out the side door. David looked back at his son and the mother of his only child. He mouthed the words, "I love you."

Casey cried and held her little son tightly. He asked, "Where is that man taking my daddy?" Tears rolled down his chubby cheeks. It was impossible for Casey to explain to her little boy that his daddy was going away for a long time because he chose to use and deal drugs.

Spineless was smiling. "Great story, isn't it? One of my favorites, for sure. Let me introduce myself. I'm Spineless, also known as Crystal Meth. I'm a cruel drug. I take control of everyone I can. It's a wonderful life!"

The assembly of terrorists cheered, "Yeah, great life, wonderful!"

The videos continued with explanations of different stories. An alcoholic slept in the shadows under a bridge. Physical abuse led to a divorce. A crack-addicted mother in a filthy house let her children eat food scraps off the floor. Children were at home alone while their single parent worked. The other parent was in prison on drug-related charges. A pretty, stylish young mother started out with a good life, but later appeared wasted with dark circles under her hollow eyes. A successful executive stood on a columned porch of a huge brick home with his beautiful wife and two children. Later, the same man was in a lunch line at a homeless mission.

Hack spoke with cruel intent. “Well, human species, you have seen our methods and the history to prove our success. You can’t see the future, but we certainly can.” He raised his fist and growled, “This is a war, and we will win by tricking stupid little kids!”

# THEY ARE COMING AFTER YOU

## The Target List

The conference was ending, and Mr. Flatulent spoke. "Now it's time for the grand finale. You will all get your assignments." The terrorists erupted in applause, screaming, and dancing.

He went on with pride. "Bring out the target list."

From backstage, the enslaved, skeletal crack rats rolled out stacks of paper. Each page had a picture of an individual or an entire family, with their addresses. Additional information included their habits and weaknesses. Each had a numerical code in the top right-hand corner. Terrorist ushers distributed them to attendees.

"There are thousands of innocent, unsuspecting kids that we can trick, trap, and addict."

"Trip, trap and addict!" the audience wildly responded.

"There is also an adult category if you want one of those stupid fools. The real ripe kids are pictured with their parents, ready for picking."

They showed the photos to each other, pointing and laughing at their assigned targets. "Wow! We're sure gonna surprise them!" they commented. "One more kid done in!"

Halfweed and the captured Nopers watched the commotion in amazement. They were shocked at the terrorists' eagerness to go out and destroy innocent lives. She wondered what had happened to the six Nopers left to guard the camera crew.

While the crowd discussed their new tasks, the research team hurried over to Hack and put a note in his hand. As he read the note, his eyes grew large, and a big smile appeared on his face until finally he began laughing uncontrollably. Hack walked with confidence to take the microphone.

He asked, "Who has photos numbered 429, 8315, and 11536?" Everyone in the audience checked their numbered pictures, and three hands shot into the air with loud affirmative responses.

"Bring them to me," Hack motioned for quick action. The three ran up the steps and across the stage to give the pictures to Hack. He studied them with his reddened eyes while they waited to see what he would do. Hack held up a picture for the camera to get a clear shot.

"Number 429. Dr. Whyze, do you recognize this young person?" Hack asked.

It was Tommy! Both Tommy and Dr. Whyze were stunned as they stared into the monitor.

"That's me, Dad! That's my picture!" Tommy backed away from the monitor. He was horrified.

Dr. Whyze feared for his son, but did not admit it. He avoided looking at Tommy so he would not see the panic in his eyes. Instead, he busied himself with the microscope and said, "It's you, Tommy. I know that, but I will keep you safe from Hack." He sounded noble enough, but he wondered if he could keep his son safe. *How can I fight the scum of the underworld when I can't see it except under a microscope? Hack said this is a war. I will fight back to keep my family safe.* Rage was boiling inside him as he thought about Hack's threats to his eleven-year-old. He wanted to slam his fist through the monitor and knock Hack beyond infinity, to some place where he could never hurt another kid.

Hack shook the picture furiously. "Do you see who this is, Dr. Whyze? Do you?" From the bottom of the picture, he read, "3036 Melba Street, eleven-year-old, white male, upper income, average intelligence, insecure about his appearance. Vulnerable and sad about his parents' divorce. Doesn't understand and wonders if the divorce was his fault. Admires his older brother who has already started smoking. Spends time in the lab with his father, but his father never has time to go to his school events. Thinks his father is weird. Feels lonely because his mother and father are both too busy with their personal interests and seldom spend time with him. Feels rejected by his mother."

"Tommy, do you think I'm weird?" Dr. Whyze was glad for the interruption in his raging thoughts. He wanted to cool down before Tommy recognized an anger burning out of control.

"No, Dad, you're really smart."

Dr. Whyze did not comment, but he felt guilty and was sad because he and Miranda had not stayed married. They had not worked together to raise their children properly after the divorce.

Hack gazed steadily and directly into the camera's lens as he continued. "Are you there, Tommy? Are you with your dad looking at me? If you are, one of our friends is coming to get you." He handed the picture back to the drug terrorist beside him, pointed to the monitor and ordered, "Go after him! He can't resist our temptation!"

Hack enjoyed holding up another picture with the same question as before. "Do you know this young boy, Dr. Whyze?"

Sitting straight up, Tommy eyed the monitor and said, "Dad, that's Mark!"

Dr. Whyze answered, "I know, Tommy. Try not to let it scare you." He had been able to bring his rage and fear under control, but it simmered again as he wondered, *How far will Hack go to stop me and Tommy from exposing the drug underworld? Is it worth the risk? It's a risk I'll have to take. I will not let scum like Hack and his cronies hurt my family or other innocent children.*

Hack read again from his photo information, "Thirteen years old, shy, started smoking to fit in with other kids, hates his appearance. Thinks his parents' divorce is his fault. Feels lonely. Since the divorce, he is raising himself because his mother is busy with her social life. Has few friends and no close friends." Hack mocked sadness and pity for him. "Not involved in school events. No discipline from parents who never monitor what he sees on TV or the internet. Parents are clueless about his friends or their families."

Tommy's big brown eyes glanced at his father, but Dr. Whyze said nothing. Tommy could see the sadness on his father's face.

Hack went on. "Dr. Whyze, your son will be easy to trap—a piece of cake! He'll be smoking weed in the very near future and won't develop socially because he'll be stoned. You're a scientist who taught Mark about bugs and molecules but not about life. You taught him about your interests, but you never took time to learn his interests. You may have the title of doctor, but you haven't earned your title of father. What makes you more ridiculous is that you think you can stop us. Wrong! So you think you're a genius? Yeah, dumb genius!" Hack laughed.

He shook his finger back and forth in the air, emphasizing each word. "Tommy, you will never stop us. Why? Because your parents never taught you to stand alone for anything. Kids follow other kids, doing what they do." Hack gasped for air, his breathing labored. All his excited talking was too much for his damaged lungs.

"Here," he said, coughing as he handing Mark's picture back to the terrorist. "He'll be easy. We'll have him trapped and addicted in no time. We tricked him when he started smoking. You, Dr. Whyze, helped us when you failed to teach him that he is important and unique. You didn't encourage him to develop his own interests. Surprise, Doc! This is a war on kids! On the way to sweet victory, we will trap a few adults as well," Hack said as he held up the third photo. "Victim Number 11536."

"Not mom!" exploded from Tommy's mouth. "Dad! They have a picture of my mom."

Dr. Whyze was startled speechless, his face pale as ashes. This was his sons' mother. How dare Hack threaten her!

Giving the best low whistle he could muster, Hack mocked, "She's pretty, Doc. Were you too dopey to keep her?"

Now reading from the photo, he informed the listeners, "Divorced, hates being alone. Husband was busy with his profession when she needed his attention. Gets drunk regularly with her friends. Hopes to find a new male companion. Stopped going to church."

Tommy's little-boy voice held an uncertainty as he said, "Mom wouldn't get drunk and use drugs, would she, Dad?"

"I hope not, Son."

"Hey, Doc, are you still listening?" Hack's voice turned their attention back to the monitor. "I'm not a genius, like you, but it seems to me while you were at work doing your research and making the big bucks, your family was falling apart." He rustled the paper photo of Miranda. "Here's proof. Best of all, you never saw it coming! You never saw what was happening with your wife and kids.

"I don't get it, Doc. How can you be so smart and dumb at the same time? Do you want to know the kids that are hard for us to trick? It's the ones whose parents set rules about time spent on video games, computers, and watching TV. It's the families who remove their ear buds, turn off their cell phones, and have dinner with their families four or five times a week. They take time to ask their kids about what's going on in their lives, what they are dealing with, instead of yammering on about their own lives. By the way, Doc, how is Mark doing? Oh, that's right, you don't know. Is he still your son? Why don't you spend some time with him? Why not go to school and ask how he's doing? That's your job as a father. Having a child doesn't make you a father. Being an example and teaching your kids the right way to live makes you a father. Some of you humans disgust me. You don't do your jobs and then you blame your kids' problems on, other kids, school, or drugs." Hack pretended to gag.

"One night Miranda will go to a party and a friend will be there with one of my partners. Her friend will tell her it's OK to smoke a joint, try a little powder or take a 'feel better' pill. Then BAM! It'll hit her like a ton of bricks, but she'll feel light as a feather. My troops will give her a high she has never experienced. And when people get high, we always take them down."

The crowd chanted excitedly in singsong fashion, "Take her down! Take her down!"

"Oh, and by the way, Doc," he finished with a raised voice, "if you think that you and Tommy can help Halfweed stop us, you are as stupid as she is!" His ugly head bobbed up and down, and he laughed until he was breathless.

"Who knows? Maybe you'll make our target list. You want to try one of my friends, Doc?" Hack pointed to the other leaders who represented various drugs. "And, FYI, Mr. Genius," sarcasm dripped from his mouth like the green slime from the pit where he lived, "some of your educated friends at the lab and university are regular customers. A few of the professors tell college and high school students there's no harm in trying us. We love educated people who promote our cause.

"Some of the human species are totally ignorant. They will destroy themselves and others because they have no moral standards. Anything goes. Guess what, Doc? We're always glad to help professors get their students on the express lane." The crowd and leaders on the stage were in a frenzy of anticipation.

"One last thing, Doc. We have no power unless you," his ugly finger jabbed toward the camera lens, "put us in your body, and then we take over your intelligent brain. Never forget that we have human friends who can take out you and your family if you interfere with our business. Do you understand, Doc? This is a dirty business. We destroy lives and could not care less who we hurt. That includes you, your kids, Miranda, and your neighborhood.

"You still there, smart guy? Look at the screen behind me." He turned and pointed to the jumbo screen. The massive crowd of humans on the screen was a hodgepodge of men and women of all nationalities and colors. Some were nicely dressed in the latest styles and others looked sick in their dirty, ragged clothes.

"Meet my distributors, Doc. Notice they are of your species. Let me warn you, do not threaten my human distributors! Do not interfere with their business. When someone interferes with their business, it becomes my business."

A human voice from the screen said, "Word on the street is you need our help. Is that right, Hack?"

"Precisely," Hack came back. "We have traitors—first time ever. And there is a human who knows w-a-a-a-y too much. Our business is to take people down, but I need you to take this one out!" Hack's hand moved in a slicing motion across his neck for emphasis.

"I have his address. He has two sons on the target list, and you can take them out as well. If necessary, you can take out his ex-wife. Will you take care of this?" Hack asked.

His distributors responded, "Don't worry, Hack, no problem. You know we will be more than happy to handle this for you. Where do they live?" Hack retrieved the picture and read their names and addresses to the human drug dealers and users.

The crazed crowd at the conference shouted with greater excitement than before, "Take him out! Take him out!" They followed Hack's plan of destruction like a bunch of programmed robots, without thinking or caring who got hurt.

"Dad, they're sending drug dealers to kill us!" Tommy could not hide from this new and powerful fear breathing down his neck. "I'm scared! What do we do?"

Dr. Whyze hugged his son and said, "We go to the police and let them take care of it. No one is going to get to you, Son."

Tommy felt better but could still feel the tingly sensation of fear. The characters on the screen looked vicious, but he knew he could rely on his father.

"The batteries in the camera are getting weak," Dr. Whyze said with concern. "I sure hope we don't lose the picture."

Hack turned back to the camera. "Well, Doc, are you ready? Is your little coward boy there with you? He sure doesn't know how to fight!"

Tommy defended himself saying, "I am not a coward!"

Dad joined in, "No, Tommy, you're not a coward, but being in a fight doesn't mean that you're brave or manly. Hack thinks calling you a coward will intimidate you into making wrong choices. Brave people are those who live by doing what is right."

Hack pointed his thumb back over his shoulder at the screen. "My human friends are coming after your family. They will take you out."

"Take him out! Take him out!" the terrorists chanted. He returned his focus to the conference. "Do you have your assignments?"

"Yes! WOK! WOK! WOK!" they shouted louder.

Turning his attention to Halfweed and the defectors, Hack asked in sarcastic sweetness, "You ready to disintegrate into nothingness?"

He then yelled at Halfweed with red-faced rage, "You are despicable for turning away from your tobacco family. But, after all, you're a mixed breed. Look at your unusual color. Was your momma a ragweed? What's wrong with you?

"Take them to the stream of waste. Pick up that camera and take it with you. I want Doc to see this," he said.

Hack instructed his terrorists to take Halfweed and her followers to the opposite direction of the water's flow. Hack wanted all of the conference attendees to see and celebrate the parade of traitors as they floated down stream to their complete destruction. It was painfully obvious that the terrorists enjoyed pushing, shoving, and dragging the Nopers. Halfweed and her followers appeared to be brave and strong as they were forced to line up at the edge of the stinking slime.

"Would any of you traitors like to change your minds and rejoin our forces?" Hack challenged.

"NO! We are not terrorists! We are Nopers!"

"Any last words, Halfweed? You are the cause of this, and you're taking these other losers with you."

"I'm glad I changed to a Noper. If I die in the sewer," she looked down at the flow of rotten human waste, "so be it. But you, your terrorists, and your human friends are all sewer scum! Kids are smarter than you think. Your empire will fail." Laughter echoed around her. Halfweed did not care. She would die before becoming a doper. "I will never follow you, Hack."

Tommy was more worried and frightened than any time in his whole life. "Dad, can you stop them? They are going to kill Halfweed! She's trying to do what is right. Can't you do something?"

"There is nothing I can do, Son. Unfortunately, those who do what is right may be laughed at and get their feelings hurt. Still, you do the right thing."

Hack raised his arms to silence the crowd. "No one will stop us. The only ones who can slow us down are kids who recognize the trap and say, 'Not me!' But no one in our own family will hinder our work and live. Enjoy watching them as they become extinct!"

The terrorists jumped for joy as they threw the Nopers into the sewer, one at a time. They saved the best for last—Halfweed.

Hack repeated to Halfweed, "You are the cause of this, you traitor." He helped his soldiers pick her up and toss her into the nasty liquid. Out of breath after using all his strength, he sat down on the edge of the pipe. He was glad to end the existence of the traitor he hated. The crowd applauded and stomped rhythmically as the traitors floated slowly out of sight to the main sewer system.

The Nopers tried to get to a dry area, but terrorists kicked and pushed them back into the stream. Their fight to live seemed hopeless. Slowly losing their strength, they lay motionless in the water.

Hack noticed the traitors were not dissolving as quickly as he thought they would. But they were out of sight, and he was confident they were gone forever.

Hack continued the most important part of the conference. "Now is your chance to show how skilled you are at trapping kids. It's time to hit the streets and accomplish your purpose!"

With the pictures of their assignments in hand, the crowd excitedly ran to the manhole exits and into the city streets of Notaware. Some shouted, "WOK! WOK! WOK!" as they quickly dispersed in all directions and their voices faded into silence.

Hack and the leaders congratulated each other on the success of the conference. As they entered the private meeting room with the Doc's camera, Tommy and his dad saw the monitor flicker and go blank. There was no picture or sound. They would always wonder what happened to Halfweed and her followers.

# A Call for Help

Dr. Whyze called the police chief's office.

"City of Notaware, Precinct 10, Chief Skeptical's office."

"My name is Dr. Whyze, and I would like to speak to the police chief."

"What's this about?" questioned the voice.

"I'm a research scientist and have discovered an underworld plot called a War on Kids. This is a wicked plan to get kids to try drugs and trap them into addiction."

The operator was stunned into silence. Finally responding, she said, "One moment please." She called the police chief's secretary, Miss Syvil.

"I've got some idiot on the phone who wants to talk to the chief."

Sounding bored with her job Miss Syvil replied, "Put him through."

"Chief Skeptical's office, may I help you?"

Dr. Whyze repeated the information.

The secretary asked, "Where did you see this plot?"

Dr. Whyze explained, "While doing research in my lab, I discovered drug particles living in the city sewer. They have a plan to trick kids into using drugs and trap them in addiction."

A chuckle escaped from the secretary's lips. "Were there any witnesses to this?"

Dr. Whyze was relieved to be able to respond, "Yes! My eleven-year-old son was with me and saw everything."

Stifling a giggle and a yawn, the secretary answered, "I understand, Sir. May I get your name and phone number? I will have the chief call you for an appointment."

Dr. Whyze protested, "Miss, you don't understand. This is urgent. The plot is being hatched even as we speak! Drug terrorists have been dispatched all over the city. I fear that my family may be in danger."

"Mister, the chief is a very busy man. I will have him call you as soon as possible."

Dr. Whyze could tell by the woman's rude reply that she thought he was a quack, but he gave her his name and phone number anyway. As he hung up the phone, he wondered if the police chief really would return his call.

Miss Syvil took the note to her boss and informed him, "This message is from a man claiming to be some kind of research scientist who has uncovered a plot to trap kids in addiction. He wants an appointment with you. He sounds crazy to me." Rolling her eyes at his ridiculous claims, she handed Chief Skeptical the note with Dr. Whyze's name and phone number.

The police chief listened closely, and though Miss Syvil thought the call insignificant, he wanted to know more. He wanted to hear from Dr. Whyze. With silent authority, he dismissed the doubting secretary and picked up the phone.

"Dr. Whyze? This is Police Chief Skeptical. Can you come in tomorrow at two p.m. to discuss the matter of the drug plot?"

"Yes! I will be there at two o'clock sharp. Thank you very much for returning my call."

Chief Skeptical, a big man with a booming voice, was a loving husband and father. He loved his six children more than anything, including his job. Sometimes he would let his children ride in the police car with him. He wanted them to know what drugs and alcohol can do to people. He would read newspaper articles to his kids and watch the news with them so he could explain how drugs and alcohol can destroy people.

He would say, "You're too valuable to destroy yourself with drugs and alcohol. You're not any better than those people. They just don't realize they are unique, special creations." His kids knew the dangers and had already made up their minds. Each one said, "I'm too valuable to destroy myself with drugs and alcohol."

Although very busy, Chief Skeptical attended most school events. He expected his kids to respect their teachers, be on time for classes, make good grades, and complete all homework assignments. His kids were responsible for cleaning their rooms and doing other household chores assigned by both parents. His motto was, "Homework and chores first, play later."

When his children misbehaved, the chief was careful not to embarrass them in public. After warning them about bad behavior, he always followed through with discipline at home. The children had to explain what they had done and why it was wrong. Afterward, they got hugs and acceptance.

Many years as police chief had gained Mr. Skeptical a reputation for being honest, tough, fair, and compassionate. He loved the kids in his city. He frequently drove through neighborhoods and talked with kids on the streets about their dreams, their schools, and their parents. Every conversation ended with, "You're a unique creation. Repeat after me, I'm one of a kind! I don't want to be a copy of someone else. I'm too valuable to destroy myself with drugs and alcohol."

He knew that many of the kids did not know who or where their fathers were. Some lived with grandparents or other relatives because their parents were divorced, some in prison or addicted. Most single moms struggled to provide for their kids because the fathers would not help. Physical, emotional, and verbal abuse were common in many families. Chief Skeptical knew that some of these kids had already thought of quitting school and might become drug dealers or addicts themselves. He often talked to kids and parents about the importance of a good education so they would not have to depend on the government to take care of them.

He was in demand as a public speaker. He spoke to school assemblies, graduations, and many public events. He would always start with, "You're too valuable to destroy yourself with drugs and alcohol. The kind of person you become is not determined by where you live, what kind of car you drive, or how much money you have. There is nothing wrong with being poor, but, but, but…" he would repeat and everyone would laugh. "If you want a better and a different life, it takes hard work! You must stay in school, get a good education, learn a trade, or go to college."

He would talk about the man he respected most. "My father worked in a grocery store. He was good at keeping the shelves stocked and in order. He knew there was not a better job in his future because he couldn't read or write very well.

"Most of our clothes were handed down from family members or bought at second-hand stores, but dad never complained. His clothes were always clean and pressed when he went to work. He would ride his bike to work if our old car wouldn't run. He took pride in being an honest, hard worker and was grateful for what we had. He wasn't ashamed that we were poor.

"We were not allowed to complain about what others had that we couldn't get. Every day we gave thanks for what we had. He insisted we do our very best and get a good education. He would say to all six of us kids, 'whatever you do, do it well and do it with pride.' My father was the best man I ever knew."

It did not matter if the people Chief Skeptical spoke to were age six or sixty. He told them how drugs and alcohol ruined so many lives in his city. He would ask the audience to repeat several times, "I'm too valuable to destroy myself with drugs and alcohol."

The next afternoon, two o'clock finally crept around. Dr. Whyze and Tommy arrived at the chief's office a few minutes early. They were both nervous, but Tommy forgot the butterflies in his stomach when he saw so many police officers wearing guns. He shrank closer to his dad when a man in hand cuffs tried to break away from an officer. *Maybe he's one of the drug dealers sent to get us*, Tommy thought.

They approached the information desk and asked where the Police chief's office was located. Following directions down the hall, Dr. Whyze lightly knocked and then entered the door labeled "Police Chief."

He introduced himself to the same doubting secretary he had spoken to on the phone. "I am Dr. Whyze. This is my son, Tommy. We have a two o'clock appointment with Chief Skeptical."

Her face held an expression of surprise. She had no idea the Chief had called Dr. Whyze about his unbelievable story.

"I'll tell the chief you're here. Please be seated until he is ready to see you."

Before they could settle in their chairs, the Chief emerged from his office with an extended hand to invite them in. He looked like a giant to Tommy, but a gentle giant. His kindness made both of them feel relaxed as they took their seats.

"Tell me about your discovery, Dr. Whyze."

Dr. Whyze began the story, but the chief immediately stopped him.

The chief looked squarely at Tommy and asked, "Did you see these characters as well, Tommy?"

Tommy's brown eyes opened wider. *Does Police Chief Skeptical think my dad is lying?* Tommy quickly and emphatically explained things were exactly as his father was claiming.

The chief listened closely. but interrupted often to ask questions. He repeated back to Dr. Whyze, "You saw this on your monitor. Did you videotape these events?"

"No, the equipment did not have the right connections."

"Do you have any evidence to prove what you are telling me is true?"

"Well, no, just our story, but both Tommy and I did see it."

"Tommy, were you with your father when he saw this?" he asked again.

"Yes!" Tommy's head bobbed up and down, "I saw everything!"

The story seemed off the charts to Police Chief Skeptical. However, Dr. Whyze and Tommy both sounded convincing.

Pointing to the city map on the wall, the Chief asked, "Can you show me where this underworld meeting took place?"

Dr. Whyze nodded. "I think so."

He pointed and confidently replied, "Here, right here is where they left the underworld to come into our city."

A frown creased the chief's brow as he said, "That's right smack dab in the middle of the city, a very busy street. Well, thanks for coming in, Dr. Whyze. I'll do some research to look for proof of this underworld."

Such an abrupt end to their meeting convinced the doctor that the chief did not believe his story. He assumed they would probably never hear from the police chief again. Dr. Whyze expressed his appreciation and shook hands with the chief.

Chief Skeptical shook Tommy's small hand and asked him, "Tommy, what will you say to someone who offers you drugs?"

Tommy found his eleven-year-old courage and answered, "Not me! It's a trap!"

A smile broke across the chief's face, "Good answer, Tommy! You know the right thing to do. Maybe you can tell other kids that using drugs is a trap."

"Yes, sir. Thank you." Tommy felt important when the chief spoke directly to him.

Dr. Whyze thought of something else. "I have one other thing I must tell you. I have a young teenage son who has already started smoking and an ex-wife who is drinking excessively. Both of them, along with Tommy, are on the target list. There is a group of drug dealers who agreed to take us out—me, our two sons, and Miranda—to stop us from exposing them."

The police chief looked puzzled. "Does 'take you out' mean what I think?"

Dr. Whyze looked worried. "I'm not sure, but those are the exact words they used. I need your help to protect my family."

The police chief saw the concern and seriousness of the situation in the eyes of the doctor. He warned Dr. Whyze, “Drug dealers are heartless and will hurt people who try to stop them or hinder their business. You be very careful.”

The entire story sounded unbelievable to the kind-hearted chief. But he did not want Dr. Whyze to know he truly did not believe their weird story.

# Halfweed Surfaces

Although Halfweed and her Nopers had prepared for the gooey water, they were surprised that they had not disintegrated. The oil-covered group floated downstream into the big outdoor pond and the sunlight. They looked around to see who had survived, and all seven of them had made it. No one had disintegrated because the water could not penetrate the coating of oil they had rubbed on themselves. The oil made it easy to free their tied hands.

They swam to the edge of the water and found a dry place to rest. All were deep in their own thoughts. They soaked up the sun and enjoyed a few moments of victory. Halfweed stared into the blue sky, wondering what her next move should be. The conference had ended, and the evil terrorists were destroying young lives. Her mind raced with ideas as she looked around at those who depended on her for answers. She knew their struggles were not over.

Ending their rest time, Halfweed gathered the Nopers and entered the pipe that led to the main sewer plant. Progress was slow because they had to walk up a steep, slippery incline. The uncertainty of Hack's location called for extreme caution as they inched along.

Halfweed had grown to love her followers who were committed to stop Hack. Her mind constantly wondered what had happened to the six she had left to guard Hack's camera crew at the cell.

Some unusual movement ahead made her curious if Hack had sent some terrorists to confirm that she and her Nopers were destroyed. She motioned for her team to hide and wait until the terrorists came to them, not knowing what the outcome might be. They waited anxiously, mentally preparing for hand-to-hand combat. Halfweed was confident they could take them if necessary.

As the little group came closer, she recognized them as fellow Nopers. They were nervously looking around, hoping to evade capture. They wondered what happened to Halfweed. *Had Hack killed her?* If they could find her, they would give her a proper burial. They would not let her rot in the sewer. She was not a sewer character like Hack.

The Nopers drifted so close to Halfweed that she could touch them. She jumped from her hiding place and yelled, "Gotcha!" They screamed and fell backward. When they realized it was Halfweed, their shock turned to joy. They were all together again. All thirteen of them had survived the ordeal.

Not one of them knew where Hack and his troops were. Perhaps they were creeping up behind them now. They hid behind a sticky wad of bubble gum to make a plan. They had to overthrow those who wanted them dead.

# Warning to Miranda and Mark

As Tommy and his dad left the police station, Tommy thought of his mom. *Does she really drink a lot of alcohol or use drugs. Will the thugs hurt her? Were they threatening her in some way? Will they hurt Mark?*

The doctor had a cell phone to his ear, waiting for an answer to stop the ringing.

"Miranda! Tommy and I need to talk with you and Mark."

"About what? I'm busy and already have plans."

"Please, Miranda, it's important. I've just left the police station and I need to speak with you and Mark."

"Is something wrong, Brian? Is Tommy OK?"

"Tommy's fine. We need to talk."

Reluctantly, Miranda agreed. "Come on over, but I don't have much time."

"Be there in a minute."

As he zigzagged through traffic, the doctor's thoughts were of Miranda and their two sons. He remembered how great their marriage was in the beginning. The two had been deeply in love and excited about the prospect of having children. Their conversations often centered on child rearing and religion. They had agreed that religion was important and selected a place of worship where they both felt comfortable. They had been determined to raise their children to live right.

When Mark was born, the couple worshipped regularly. Though they were busy with work, activities, and friends, they made a habit of sharing the day's events around the dinner table most evenings. After Tommy was born, more responsibility followed. Their busy lives made it easy to skip worshipping together. Family time became less frequent and dinner together less of a priority. Without their evening talks, the family drifted apart.

Just like his dad, Tommy was deep in thought. He remembered his parents' disturbing arguments. Most of the time the subject was money, but often he and Mark were at the center of the loud commotions. Tommy entered kindergarten at the age of five, confused about why his parents disliked each other so much.

A year later, both parents sat down with their sons and broke the news that they were getting a divorce. Tommy and Mark both thought the divorce might be their fault. Arguments over money for school, clothes, and medical bills were mostly about them and their needs. Besides, Mom and Dad had important careers. They had little time for kids.

A simple legal process ended the marriage, and the once-loving spouses went their separate ways. They agreed to divide the little money they had and made the necessary living arrangements. Dr. Whyze thought he should stay in the house to have access to his lab. Since Miranda hated the lab, this was not a problem for her. Many of their arguments had been about all the time the doctor spent in the lab, not with her.

The boys knew they could always find their dad in the lab, and he was happy to let them observe his activities. Trouble was, Mark had no interest in scientific stuff, and Tommy, even with his keen interest in his dad's work, became bored with hours of looking into a microscope. Perhaps things would have been different if there had been some fun in the mix, or even a few long conversations, but that was not the case.

Dr. Whyze pulled his SUV into the parking lot of the apartment complex. The grounds were pleasant, with pink crape myrtles and yellow blooming hyacinths. Tommy was out of the car before the engine was off. His mother met him at the door, somewhat caught off guard by his huge, spontaneous hug. Mark emerged from his room and spoke to them. Dr. Whyze gave Mark an informal, one-arm hug, but the former husband and wife barely acknowledged each other. Since the divorce, they had been kind to one another, but there was absolutely no affection between them, not even caring words.

Tommy and Mark pulled sodas from the fridge and went into the living room of the nice apartment. The adults sat on the sofa, coffee cups in hand, with Tommy seated between them. Mark stood in the doorway, wanting to be left out of whatever was going on.

"Mark, you need to listen to this. Come sit down." Mark obeyed, but plopped down in the big armchair and muttered something rude under his breath.

"Brian, what's going on? What did you report to the police?" Miranda sounded concerned but irritated that her ex was taking time from her busy day. *He had years to spend time with me and chose not to*, she thought resentfully. But in spite of his weirdness, she knew he was a good man. She felt a little guilty for her anger toward him. As Dr. Whyze repeated the wild tale of the drug underworld, a look of disbelief registered on Miranda's face.

"All of it's true, Mom. I saw it!" Tommy said in a high-pitched voice tinged with a protective edge, in case she thought that he and his dad had made it up.

"Miranda, there is something more serious that you need to know. You, Mark, and Tommy are all targets for attack, to be tempted with drugs."

"I won't use drugs!" she said loudly defending herself. "Mark is too smart to even consider it, and Tommy's only eleven years old."

Tommy blasted back, "They have a picture of you, Mom, and say you get drunk all the time. They said that soon someone will offer you drugs and you'll try that too."

Irritated with her young son, Miranda harshly shot back, "That's foolishness! I would never touch the stuff. I do have a few drinks on occasion, but I don't get drunk all the time."

The doctor's eyes pleaded with her to believe him. "Mark is on the list because he has already started smoking and hanging out with the wrong crowd. He's headed for trouble, Miranda. Dealing with this later may be too late."

Mark stared at his dad in silence, but the smirk on his face said much more than words.

Tommy jumped up. "It's true, Mark! I tried to tell you before about their trick to get you to smoke. You just laughed and made fun of me. You're trapped, Mark!" Tears streamed down his freckled face, and he trembled in panic.

Mark wondered if Tommy's emotional outburst was caused by fear or anger. Either way, it made him feel so uneasy that he wanted to walk away. *I could use a cigarette right now to calm my own nerves. Maybe I am trapped.*

Instead of leaving, he behaved like his rebellious, smart-aleck friends. "That's so lame, Tommy! Your problem is looking into that microscope too much. It's made you crazy like Dad!" Mark's sarcastic words hit his little brother like a solid punch in his stomach.

"Why would Tommy be on that list at such a young age, Brian? None of this makes sense." Miranda had a confused look on her face. Dr. Whyze knew, she did not realize kids of all ages get hooked on drugs and some experiment with them when they are very young.

He explained, "Kids from broken homes might blame themselves for their parents' divorce. They feel sad and hurt but don't have anyone to talk to about it. It's easy for them to think drugs will make them feel better, so they become major targets of the drug underworld."

"Sheer stupidity, Brian! Kids from all families try drugs. I think you need some psychiatric help yourself. Looking in that microscope has made you crazy, and it's making Tommy go bonkers."

Feeling frustrated, he ignored her comments and got right to the point. "I know kids from all environments can be tricked by drugs, but please listen to me. Tommy and I know about the drug underworld, and dealers have been instructed to take us out."

"What does that mean, Brian? Did you really hear someone say that?"

Tommy, now in control of his emotions, interrupted. "Mom, we saw it on the screen at their underworld conference."

Miranda held up her palms toward them. "Hold up a minute! Let me get this straight. You put a tiny camera in the sewer—you did say the sewer, didn't you? And you saw these itty bitty drug characters telling dealers to hurt our family?"

"Yes, Miranda, we saw them and heard them. That is why I talked to Chief Skeptical. He has heard the whole story."

"Yeah, right. And I guess he said, 'Sure, I believe you. Officers will be dispatched immediately to the sewer.' " Her mocking smirk annoyed him.

"He said he would look into the matter; however, like you, he probably did not believe us."

"Hello!? Do you know how ridiculous this sounds, Brian? No one is going to believe this garbage. What's wrong with you?"

Tommy sprang up from the sofa, angry sparks in his brown eyes, "It's true, Mom, just like Dad said. I saw it!"

Miranda looked at him, wondering if he had emotional damage from his father's crazy imaginations. "Don't raise your voice at me, young man!"

The eleven-year-old cowered down a bit. "I'm sorry, Mom," he muttered, then added, "but it is true." He sank his small frame back into the sofa.

Dr. Whyze warned her, "I can't force you and Mark to believe this, but I do want you to be careful and watch out for each other." He realized there was nothing more to say. Believing him was a choice they would each have to make. Feeling defeated, he got up to leave. "I just hope the police will do something."

Miranda walked to the door with her former husband and youngest son. "Brian, does 'take them out' mean what I think it means?"

Was it possible that she did believe him? He slowly nodded yes, opened the door, and left. Both father and son were quiet in the car. They knew neither Miranda nor Mark believed the story. *But she did ask what "take them out" means*, Dr. Whyze recalled. A faint flicker of hope stirred. His family was in danger, and under the present circumstances, he felt unsure of what to do. His instinctive desire was to protect them. He didn't want Tommy to live in fear but knew he was already afraid.

"Hey, Tommy, let's go to your favorite restaurant and then a movie. I think we need a break and some fun."

The strained look on Tommy's face turned into a smile. "That would be fun, Dad, let's go!" he agreed in admiration for his dad. As they turned the corner, Tommy saw Sizzlin Sam's neon sign. Tommy enjoyed his favorite meal of a hamburger, curly fries, and ice cream topped with gummy worms. He felt content and happy as they walked toward the theater entrance.

Dr. Whyze wanted time to think and plan while Tommy watched the movie. He turned off his cell phone and reclined in the cushioned theater seat. Looking over at his son, he wondered how in the world he could eat popcorn and cola after the meal he had just consumed. *Kids never cease to amaze me,* he thought. Soon he was lost in his own thoughts. Tommy was lost in popcorn and the super-hero action.

# Criminals at Tommy's House

Dinner and the movie helped ease the tension in Dr. Whyze and Tommy, but it did not last. When they turned onto Melba Street, they were shocked to see red and blue lights flashing in front of their house. As soon as they parked in the driveway, the police chief stepped out of his cruiser and walked toward their old blue SUV.

Dr. Whyze stepped out of the car and asked, "Why are you here? Has something happened? Is Miranda OK? Is Mark in trouble? Has something happened to them?" Tommy heard the panic rise in his dad's voice. His own little heart thumped faster.

"Calm down, your family is OK. No one is in trouble. However, your residence has been broken into. Neighbors called us when they noticed two cars repeatedly circling the block and slowing in front of your house. When we got here, they were gone. The neighbors were unable to get the license plate numbers, but they did give us a good description of the vehicles. Whoever it was ransacked your house and did plenty of damage."

As they walked into the house, the doctor and Tommy froze in the doorway, stunned by what they saw. Every piece of furniture was overturned. Shattered glass, family photos, ripped sofa cushions, and other wreckage covered the floor.

Tommy ran to his room to discover clothes and toys scattered about. He saw his favorite Spiderman shirt shredded to bits. His old and trusted GI Joe was nowhere in sight. Where was his collection of cars? Had they been stolen? He had no idea how to react. He stood and stared in stunned silence until his father's hand on his shoulder helped him finally speak.

"Why would someone do this, Dad?" His pale face twisted with anger, and his large dark eyes held fear and pain.

"Only those who did it can answer that question. We'll get through this together, Son." He gently but firmly turned his frightened son away from the disarray. Tommy gave no resistance and walked with his dad back through the jumbled mess.

The thugs had hit every room in the house. The usually neat kitchen was a heap of broken dishes from the emptied cabinets and food from the still-open refrigerator. A running faucet in the bathroom sink had flooded the room and was now flowing down the hallway. *It looks like a tornado touched down in every room of this house,* Brian thought angrily. Tommy never asked the question but wondered who in the world would clean up the mess.

"Will you be able to find the intruders?" Dr. Whyze asked the police chief.

"I hope they all go to jail and stay forever!" Tommy stomped his foot.

"Officers have been sent to your wife's apartment. She knows your house was vandalized. Unmarked police cars are stationed throughout the apartment complex to watch for suspicious activity."

"Thanks, Chief. Do you have any idea why someone would do this?"

"We have no leads at this time, although there is a possibility it is connected with the story you told me earlier. There's something in your lab you need to see."

"Oh, no! They did not destroy my lab, did they?" Distressed, he ran his fingers through his hair.

"I'm sorry, sir, but yes, they did, possibly even worse than your house."

Tommy and the chief followed close behind as Dr. Whyze hurried to the lab. They cautiously stepped around splintered glass and entered through the broken door. To their horror, expensive microscopes and research equipment lay demolished on the floor. The doctor was speechless. His eyes shifted to the bare wall where large cabinets that held chemicals and small tools had been overturned. They were horrified at the sight of words written on the wall in blood-red lipstick, "WE WILL TAKE YOU OUT!"

"This is alarming, Doctor. These are the words you heard from the drug underworld." There were still undertones of skepticism in the chief's voice. After all, Dr. Whyze was a little strange, and he wondered if the doctor himself could have plotted the whole scheme.

"Yes, it is alarming," he replied in a flat tone of voice. Shock had drained him of emotion. "It is exactly what they said. You know as

well as I do what that could mean. This is not an empty threat. It's just the beginning of a much more serious crime."

The chief answered his ringing phone. After a pause, he said, "Hold them. We'll be there as quickly as possible.

I need you and Tommy to come with me. My officers picked up three suspicious-looking males and a female circling the parking lot of your wife's apartment building. One of you might recognize them." They walked out the door and across the lawn to the cruiser at the curb.

"Tommy, you get in the front seat. Your dad won't mind riding in the back." The chief opened the passenger side door, and the little boy's cheeks reddened with exhilaration as they sped off with the siren screaming. Cars pulled to the side to let the police car pass. For a few minutes, Tommy was not a frightened eleven-year-old who had become the target of a crime. He felt like a deputy to Chief Skeptical. "Dad, this is so cool. I want to be a police officer when I grow up. OK, Dad?"

When they arrived at Miranda's apartment complex, Tommy yelled, "Hey, Dad, look!" He pointed out the handcuffed suspects sitting on the curb. The patrol car's headlights highlighted them as neighbors stood around whispering among themselves about what might have happened.

"Dr. Whyze, do you recognize any of these people? Tommy, have you ever seen them?" Chief Skeptical asked. "Were any of these in the group instructed to take you out?"

Feeling important, Tommy swung his short legs to the ground and stepped out of the police car. Dr. Whyze placed his hand on his son's shoulder. As they closely inspected the young hooligans, the doctor noticed that the female wore no lipstick, but the blood-red blotches on her shirt matched the color of the writing on his lab wall.

"The officer that stopped them found alcohol, drugs, and drug paraphernalia in the vehicle. It's obvious they are drug users," Chief Skeptical commented.

Dr. Whyze commented, "None of them look familiar to me."

"I don't remember seeing any of them," Tommy agreed.

Chief Skeptical ordered the officers to take them to the station and put them in lockup until he arrived for the interrogation. "It may be a while," he told them. "I need to take the doctor and his boy home."

"Could you hold up just a sec, Chief?" Dr. Whyze asked. "I need to talk with Miranda and Mark before we leave here." Without waiting for an answer, he pulled them to the side for privacy. "Miranda, are you and Mark OK?"

"Yes, I think so. This is all so confusing and scary. I wonder if these four young people would have really hurt us."

"I'm sorry, Miranda, but I just don't have many answers for you. I'm not sure what is going on, but I do think they are connected with the sewer underworld." Dr. Whyze assumed he was the cause of his family being in danger.

Miranda shook her head to clear the confusion and doubt she felt. "None of that stuff makes any sense, Brian. I just don't buy it."

He looked at her, wishing she could believe him. "I understand that it makes no sense to you. But Tommy and I saw it, Miranda. I firmly believe it was those four kids who broke into my house and laboratory."

"How much damage was done?" she asked.

"They destroyed nearly everything in the house and the lab, and they would have done the same thing here if the chief had not suspected something was up."

"That's terrifying!" she answered. "Mark, we need to go back inside now. Tommy, you should stay here with us tonight. You'll be safer here for the night."

"No thanks, Mom," Tommy refused. "I want to go with Dad."

"Brian, could you help me out here? He is not safe at your place. At least we weren't broken into."

"Miranda, you know I would never let anything happen to Tommy. He'll be all right with me. If he wants to come with me, let him."

She stared at both of them with concern. Her intense blue eyes held Tommy and his father in place until she finally nodded her silent consent.

"You get in the front seat this time, Dad," Tommy offered as they got into the police chief's car.

"I think I will, Son. Thanks. Buckle up back there."

"Yes, sir, I will."

As they slowly drove back to their neighborhood, Dr. Whyze asked the chief, "Did you see the red blotches on the woman's clothes?"

"Yes. I think we may have caught the vandals. Frankly, I was hoping it was the drug dealers you described."

Some of the stress eased from Dr. Whyze's face before he answered, "I believe there is a connection. The truth will be discovered."

Tommy's eyes never left the blinking lights on the car's dash, but his ears absorbed every word spoken between the two men.

"Do you want to stay at home tonight?" Chief Skeptical asked the doctor. "Perhaps you would you feel safer in a hotel?"

"Home," the doctor answered without hesitation. "I won't let drug addicts and dealers rob us of our home or stop my research."

"Do you realize how dangerous this can be?" the chief asked. "Sane people will do crazy things under the influence of drugs. They will steal, hurt innocent people, even kill to get what they need. Cold, hardhearted dealers are the worst. They care about no one but themselves."

"I'll take my chances, Chief."

"All right, Doc, if you're sure. I'll have an officer watch your place and Miranda's."

"Thank you, Sir. I'm sure we will all sleep better knowing a policeman is right outside."

The black and white car pulled into the drive. Father and son said good night to the officer and watched as he backed slowly out of the driveway. As they walked to their front door, Chief Skeptical flashed his lights at the unmarked car parked across the street.

When they opened the front door, Dr. Whyze wondered how a grown man could feel so overwhelmed. He felt as small as the eleven-year-old who depended on him for protection. Tommy looked around. Fear made his throat feel tight, like he couldn't breathe.

"Dad, are you scared?"

"Yes, a little, Son," Dr. Whyze said evasively. "More than that, though, I am exhausted."

Working together, they moved some of the debris around to find a place to sleep. As they lay down together, Tommy felt safe beside his dad. Before sleep overtook them, they wondered what would happen the next day.

# Sabrina Tells All

The next morning came early for Chief Skeptical. He was eager to question the young suspects arrested the night before. All four had criminal records for drug possession with the intent to distribute. Two of the young men had armed robbery charges and were currently on probation. These new violations of the law could easily send them to prison.

The chief's first stop was the coffee pot. As he poured the steaming, brown liquid into his favorite mug, he wondered how difficult the interrogation would be. Would the suspects resist? Would they lie? He hoped for the truth but thought his expectations might be too high considering who these people were.

The interrogation room, surrounded with large windows and

mirrors, held only a metal table and chairs. Chief Skeptical was particularly interested in the female's version of what happened. The only piece of evidence the police found belonged to the female.

"Recognize this, Sabrina?" A soft click sounded in the silent room as the chief placed a gold lipstick case on the gray metal table in front of her.

"Yeah, what about it?" the sullen female responded.

He pulled off the top and twisted the near-empty tube, eying the scuffed, red remains inside. Sabrina knew there was no way out. She may as well confess. He had matched it to the red message on Dr. Whyze's lab wall. Tears streamed down her face. Her fingers twisted nervously around each other. Chief Skeptical put a box of tissues in front of her, but was not swayed by her tears. The trapped woman was visibly afraid, unable to sit still. Her legs bounced and twitched nervously under the table.

"I only wrote it because they told me to. They said if I didn't, they would hurt me. I knew they meant it because it's happened before."

"Who told you? And why those particular words?"

"The drug dealers," Sabrina sniffed. "They promised us free drugs if we would terrify the doc and his family. They told us to 'take them out.' When we got there, no one was home so we tore up the house and lab, and left the message on the wall."

"Who told you to take them out? Who gave you the drugs? Names, Sabrina, I want names!"

Hoping the chief would go easy on her if she cooperated, Sabrina gave him what he wanted. As she named those responsible, the chief wrote them down on a note pad. Some were nicknames, but the chief had enough information to locate the known gang leaders and drug dealers.

Early the next day the chief phoned Dr. Whyze and asked him to come with Tommy to the station to identify the suspects. Eight men lined the wall behind a one-way mirror, each holding a numbered sign.

"There's no reason to be nervous, Tommy. You can see them, but they can't see you." The chief had one hand on Tommy's shoulder to comfort him while the other hand pointed to the protective mirror between them and the suspects.

"Do either of you recognize any of these people? Remember, they can't see you."

Tommy stared wide-eyed through the glass. His small carrot-top head shook back and forth to indicate he did not recognize any of them. He looked up at his father, who was studying each face carefully.

The police chief remained uncertain about Dr. Whyze's story. In an effort to test him, he had filled the first lineup with employees of the police department.

Finally, Dr. Whyze shook his head and said, "No, none of them were there."

"I have eight more I want you to see," the chief said. They waited while officers escorted the first eight men out of the room. The next line-up had six males and two females. Each held a number to his or her chest. Dr. Whyze responded immediately this time.

"That's them. Numbers two, five, six, and eight. The one in the red shirt was the main spokesman."

"Numbers one, three, four, and seven are free to go," the chief spoke. Four other men filled in the empty spaces.

Dr. Whyze said quickly, "Yes, all eight were there. I remember each one."

"Are you sure?" Chief Skeptical asked.

"Yes, yes, I'm sure! I studied and memorized their faces when I realized these men were told to take us out. I would recognize them anywhere." He looked directly into the chief's eyes when he said it. Now Chief Skeptical was convinced.

The chief turned to Tommy and asked, "Do you recognize them, Son?"

Tommy stared at them. They were so real now—not on video, but alive and standing right in front of him. If not for the glass between them, he could reach in and touch them, or they could reach out and . . . Fear made him feel sick in his stomach. He felt his heart pounding. When he tried to speak, the words did not come out. He wanted to turn and run, but choked back his fear and nodded.

"Tommy, I didn't hear what you said." The chief's voice sounded distant to him.

"Yes, sir, I think they are the ones," he squeaked out. There! He said it and they were still on the other side of the glass. Not one of them had budged so much as an inch. No huge hand smashed through the glass to smack him and hurl his skinny little body across the room. The pounding behind his eyes slowed, and his ears stopped burning. It was over at last. Scrawny though he was, he had lived through it. He looked down at his bony body. *I gotta eat more.* He looked again at the thugs behind the one-way glass and turned away.

Chief Skeptical patted them both gently and complimented, "Good job!" He added, "The men in the last lineup are all known drug addicts and dealers. We got their names from the four suspects picked up last night. They confessed to receiving drugs as payment to take you out. When they didn't find you at home, they vandalized your house and lab and left their red warning on the wall. Since the lipstick matched the threatening message, they knew they were caught."

"Thanks, Chief. I sure appreciate it. I don't want Miranda or Mark to get hurt. Do you think my family is safe now?"

Tommy studied his dad's face. His young mind questioned, *why wouldn't we be safe now? We just identified the drug-dealing thugs.*

"Probably not," Chief Skeptical answered. "Oh, I'll lock them up and charge them with a crime, but the law says they are innocent until proven guilty at a trial. Some of these criminals think they are smarter than the police. Most of them have to act tough because they are really afraid and insecure. They follow others without even thinking. Eventually, they may all go to prison, but I can't keep the dealers and gang members in jail. I will have to release them. There's no proof of an actual crime. No judge or jury would ever believe the story of a drug underworld in the sewer.

"You and Miranda need to be extra cautious. Keep your doors locked and notice your surroundings inside and out. Never assume you and your family are safe until this is all settled. I'll keep you fully informed, Doc. I have loads of work to do now, but call if you need me."

The chief walked down the hall toward his office, then turned and called back to Tommy. "Tommy, if you are offered drugs what will you say?"

Tommy grinned and boldly said, "Not me! It's a trap!" The chief raised two thumbs up.

Dr. Whyze took Tommy's hand and headed for the nearest exit. He looked down at his son who seemed so small in the middle of crime and criminals. He had thought that identifying the suspects would relieve his stress and fear. He breathed a long, deep sigh, realizing relief was nowhere in sight. *I cannot let the thugs intimidate me! I won't let them intimidate me. Now is no time to give in to fear. I have to protect my family. Those no-goods will not hurt us or get the best of me.* He could feel anger burning in his chest.

"Dad, you're hurting my hand." Tommy pulled his small hand out of his dad's tight grip.

"Sorry, Son." Tommy knew it was unintentional. He looked up at him, wondering what he had been thinking. *Does my dad think someone might grab me and run? I sure don't want to get kidnapped. Is that why he squeezed my hand so tight?* Tommy could not stop thinking about thugs and drugs and creepy criminals. It frightened and confused him. He slid into the car seat wishing he could scoot all the way over to his dad. But he snapped his seatbelt and sat in silence.

On the drive to Miranda's, Dr. Whyze spoke encouraging words to Tommy. He praised him for his bravery and assured him they were safe, yet cautioned him to be a little more careful for a while. Tommy listened quietly. He wanted to feel safe again.

The SUV wheeled into the parking lot. Eager to see his mom, Tommy got to her door first and rang the bell.

"Who is it?" came the voice on the other side of the door.

"It's me, Mom."

Miranda opened the door and looked into her son's face. Her gentle mom-smile made Tommy glad he was there. He hugged her in that quick way that only little boys can. She looked out the door past Tommy, wishing his skinny arms were still around her.

"Did you drive yourself?"

Tommy laughed. "No, Mom! Dad's coming."

She heard her ex-husband's quick steps coming up the sidewalk and opened the door wider. As soon as he was inside, Dr. Whyze shut the door and locked it.

"What's going on, Brian? Why are you two here so early? We were just having breakfast if you want to join us."

"I'm starved," Tommy said as he headed for the kitchen. He realized that the fear he had swallowed was no longer filling his stomach. The emptiness left in its place growled for waffles and syrup.

"Coffee sure smells good, Miranda. Maybe I will have something." She saw his weariness.

The four of them discussed the events of the busy morning over breakfast, the first meal and conversation they had shared in months. There was no talk about family restoration. When breakfast and their discussion of vandals and thugs were over, members of the small family went their separate ways.

# CAN YOU SEE THE TRAP?

## Halfweed Barricades Hack

The Nopers remained determined to stop Hack from damaging more humans, though they were uncertain how to do it. Energized by their purpose, they continued the journey through the sewer pipe. A calm and assertive Halfweed signaled for silence as the small group neared Hack's meeting place. The gushing noise of the water helped conceal their presence.

Sewer rats, desperately looking for food, eyed them hungrily as they floated by. Prickles of fear crawled up the spines of Halfweed's faithful little crew. She was afraid, but her desire to stop Hack was greater than all her fear.

The fidgety rats were entirely dependent on Hack to support their drug addictions. They were a pitiful, disgusting sight, literally wasting away. The rats waited, hoping Hack would give them another fix, but he had no more need for them. Hack was a typical drug dealer. He exploited the drug addicts, then pushed them aside and forgot about them. He had used the rats to build his conference center, but now they were weak and no longer productive.

Halfweed recalled things she had told the Nopers. The only difference between nicotine and other drugs is that cigarettes are legal, but they are just as addictive. What happened to these rats is precisely what happens to human beings. They think smoking is cool and they become enslaved to a smoking stick. Halfweed thought of the dependable few standing behind her. This is a good lesson for them.

They all scurried up the wall to a perfect observation site. Through a hole, they could see the entire meeting room where the drug leaders were gathered. They could hear everything as it echoed off solid concrete walls—every word clear as a bell.

The governing body of the drug underworld sat at a big executive table with Hack at the head. No one entered the room without permission. Their servants were drug terrorists who quickly responded to any order. As the leaders chatted about the success of the conference, one stood up with a glass in his hand. Raising it toward Hack, he said, "A toast to Hack for another great conference."

A second leader rose from his chair, held his glass high, and said, "A toast for the destruction of Halfweed and the Nopers."

"Hurrah! Down with Halfweed," the group shouted victoriously and turned their glasses up to drink the sparkling liquid.

Hack responded, "My greatest pleasure was to watch that group of spineless traitors float to the end of the sewer, never to live again."

"Let's watch the replay," Hack said. A camera operator inserted the DVD. They all laughed and clapped as they watched the Nopers and Halfweed topple helplessly into the sludge. They particularly enjoyed seeing terrorists kick them back as they struggled to get to the edge of the stream for safety. The video ended, and the leaders got down to business.

Old and scarred from chemical burns, Hack was not a pleasant sight to look at, yet every eye was on him. He opened with his usual boast, "We are the door to human stupidity." Hack went on, "We all understand clearly that most illegal drug users started with smoking, including the underage and irresponsible drinkers."

Of course, the other drug particles knew that was true, and if

they worked as a team, they could damage more humans. Oh, the pleasure they felt every time they saw a human fumble for a cigarette, craving the nicotine. How they loved it!

Not a single bloodshot eye moved from Hack as he continued. "We had our most successful conference ever. Now is the time to plan for our next one, but until then, we will work hard to trick innocent, unsuspecting kids. Ha! You gotta love it! Our goal is to establish camps of Devious Forces around the whole world. The human species is too stupid to recognize the danger right in front of their eyes." A smirk curled his dry, cracked lips.

"Modern technology is a wonderful tool for our cause. This conference has been simulcast around the country, and we have it on DVD for those who didn't see it live. Don't you love that! It will be sent special delivery to the entire underworld."

After pausing to cough for several minutes, Hack went on to say, "Every kid will be under the power of our plan, subject to being tricked, trapped, and . . ."

"Addicted!" the powerful leaders yelled enthusiastically.

"Listen up!" Hack spoke as loudly as he could to regain the attention of the restless group. "We can refine our skills and expand our influence on the internet. Most adults don't monitor their kids, and there are all kinds of things on the internet that can warp kids' minds."

"I think we should put an ad on the internet."

"What would it say?" Hack asked.

"Ignorance is not illegal. Come try us."

"Oh, that's funny." the entire group cracked up laughing.

"I have one: If you want to lose your money, morals, and self-respect, drugs are just what the doctor ordered." That one brought big belly laughs.

Sarcastically, one of them said, "You want to be a slave? You want to enroll in stupid? Come let us introduce you to drugs."

Hack said, "We all needed a good laugh. Let's rest a while, then work on the plans for our next conference."

Halfweed and the small group of Nopers listened intently.

"They are ruthless!" Halfweed whispered through clenched teeth. She was furious. "They take advantage of the rich and poor alike and don't care about anyone."

Her voice broke with a mix of sadness and anger. Throwing her hands up in frustration, she said, "The mentally challenged and emotionally ill are almost powerless to resist their influence. How could they?" She pointed to the conference room. "Those scheming, brutal thugs have no mercy and no conscience. They target the disadvantaged and weakest humans.

"And that's not all," she continued to express her outrage, "some humans have become like them. Can you believe that? It's common for humans to manufacture and sell drugs. They become coldhearted with no conscience. As long as they make money, they couldn't care less who they hurt. There is nothing lower than drug dealers. We have to stop them!"

She wanted to motivate her handful of followers into action and said, "We'll seal this room to trap them! We can prevent them and their ideas from ever escaping."

The handful of Nopers eagerly agreed and asked loudly, "How can we seal them in there? Tell us what to do!"

"Shush!" She raised her palm toward them. "Do you want Hack to discover us and trap us in there? Quiet!"

She spoke softly, "Here's the plan. We will recruit the rats. Hack has cut off their drug supply, so I bet they will help us. We have to work hard and fast."

"Will we ever be able to leave the sewer?" Curiosity whispered. The Nopers realized that the more they wanted to do what is right, the more repulsed they were by the sewer life. They wanted to get out of that dark, dangerous tunnel as soon as possible.

Halfweed heard a few anxious comments. "This nasty place smells disgusting and makes me want to puke. If we stay here a long time, the sewer might start to feel normal. I don't want to be like Hack and his terrorists."

She soothed their fears. "Those who never change their wrong behaviors feel perfectly normal living the sewer-life, but when you desire to do right things, the sewer no longer feels like home. You are right to recognize that drug life is the lowest form of life. Dealers are like serial killers and terrorists. We will soon leave their deadly world."

They listened closely as she explained the plan. "We will collect all the baggies used to hold drugs and use them to seal the room. It's a dirty job, so be careful. Now get busy!"

The little group launched a new vessel into the filthy water to collect as many baggies as they could. Danger was everywhere. If one of them tumbled overboard, the smelly slop would drag them away. They carefully helped each other and did not complain about the hard work. They returned over and over to stack baggies at the water's edge.

Speaking with authority, the confident Halfweed instructed the sewer rats, "Fill these bags with trash." The rats obeyed and worked quickly. Soon the bags were stuffed full. Halfweed and the Nopers were thankful for the rats because the bags were too heavy for their tiny bodies to lift.

"Now, quietly line up the bags near every opening." She had done her homework, and no hole had gone unnoticed. "We will catch them off guard and get them all at one time. Hack and his followers will have no escape route!"

Halfweed directed the rats, "Wait for my command, then move quickly, all at the same time. Stuff the bags into every hole, and make sure there is no space for escape. But the hole at the top needs to remain open. Do you understand?" The miserable rats all gave dull nods.

"Get ready. Go!"

The rats picked up heavy bags of trash and made their way to the wall. They plugged all the openings except for one at the top.

Hack was shocked as he watched every hole close up, all at the same time. *What's going on?* As the room darkened, all of them panicked and looked around for some way out. Then one of them pointed to it—the opening at the top of the room. The drug leaders pushed and shoved their way up the walls toward the only way of escape. They were all so selfish that they would not help each other. Some tumbled to the floor, then scrambled toward the opening again, yelling, "You won't trap me!"

The hole at the top of the room was larger than Halfweed thought, and terrorists escaped like ants when their mound is disturbed. Hack's bodyguards hurried to his side to help him escape.

"Stop them! Stop them now!" Halfweed shouted harshly at the rat nearest the hole. *Why isn't that rat moving?* she wondered as she saw him slumped over a heavy bag of trash. *Did he change his mind about helping? Oh, now I know! His wasted body is too weak from drug use. He can't move the big bag by himself! What do I do?*

"Hey!" Halfweed shouted to the other rats. "Get over here and help him. He can't do it alone." Without hesitation, rats rushed toward the bag, popping terrorists in their hungry mouths as they ran.

Pandemonium ruled. Just as the rats lifted the bag, Halfweed saw Hack and his body guards slip out of the opening.

"Throw them back in the room!" she shouted. The hungry rats wanted to swallow the terrorists clinging to their teeth, but they spit them through the hole. At the same time, they grabbed Hack and the bodyguards and flung them into the room that would become their prison.

Terrorists bullied the rats like just like always. "We'll get you! You'll pay for this, you low-life addicts! We will kill you if you don't die first from addiction." Strangely, the rats did not back down, but seemed to gain strength from their threats.

"Wait!" Halfweed ran toward them with something in her hand. "Don't seal the hole yet." She balanced on the edge of the hole and looked down on the leaders of the Devious Forces. They were sprawled in odd positions where they had crash landed. All of them shivered with fear and looked helplessly up at her. The little half weed that hated them was now in control.

She spoke clearly to make sure they heard every word. "You are the lowest things in the world. I may not be able to stop your friends, but I can certainly stop you." She pointed down at them, lost her balance, and almost slid in the hole. All eyes were fixed on Halfweed. After what seemed like forever, she regained her balance and tossed something into the room. It was the DVD she had recorded when held captive by the very ones she now looked down on. The terrorists cringed and covered their ears when she yelled, "I hope you enjoy the movie!"

She motioned to the rats. "OK, guys, plug it up! They will never get out of there." Obediently, the rats sealed the last exit. With a huge smile on her face, Halfweed clenched her fists and raised her arms in victory. The Nopers and the rats followed her to the edge of the water and listened as she addressed them all.

"The evil drug terrorists got exactly what they deserved. They are trapped!" She slapped her palms together with a loud pop that made them all jump. "But we can be proud of ourselves because we made right choices. Each of us decided, 'Not me! I won't be trapped, and I'm not willing to hurt others!' "

Tiny Nopers danced around Halfweed and cheered, "Not me! Not me!"

Curiosity asked Halfweed, "Will the water run clear now?"

"No, this will always be the sewer. It will never change, but we can change."

She turned to the rats and thanked them for their help. "Sewer life is not the only life there is. You don't have to be slaves. You can stay drug free and help others do the same. Come with us. Help us stop this war on kids!"

The rats decided the best way they could help was to stay and make sure Hack and the terrorists could not escape. Halfweed and her small, faithful team of warriors knew they needed to go help Tommy. She had memorized his address from the hit list. It took a long time for them to crawl up the pipe and exit through a street drain. They were thankful to be out of the filthy sewer forever. Their trip would be difficult, traveling on buses, cars, and human bodies to get to Tommy's house, but it was the right choice.

# Drug Terrorists Storm the City

Shouting "Go get 'em," thousands of terrorists burst out from the sewer system onto the city streets like horses at the start of a race. They were determined to follow their WOK orders—trick and trap kids into addiction. They ran in every direction, attacking everywhere at once. There was no place and no kid exempt from their wicked plans.

A large troop of terrorists arrived at Tommy's school with Impulse leading the way. He instructed his followers to go home with their assigned kids and report to him in the morning. The group that was appointed to Tommy's classroom gathered atop a bookshelf. They pointed and whispered, identifying their assignments. They were shocked to see Tommy sitting in his chair. Humans had been instructed to take him out, but there he was.

They climbed down the shelf, across the floor, and up the legs and arms of every student. Each terrorist settled on the shoulder of a child. This was the best position to communicate their lies. Lethargic positioned himself on the shoulder of his assigned student—Tommy.

# Police Chief Skeptical Visits Tommy

The next day, Chief Skeptical called Dr. Whyze to inform him that the suspected drug dealers were released. He was concerned about the safety of the doctor's family.

"I will have officers watching Miranda's apartment and your house. I hope we can pick up the drug dealers and gang members for another crime and keep you safe. I'll call Miranda to let her know."

"Thanks, Chief. I hope it works and my family will be safe," Dr. Whyze said apprehensively.

Chief Skeptical was sorry he had to let them go and told the doctor, "I hope you understand, Dr. Whyze. I know much of your story is true, but a jury would never believe the reason why you could identify the drug dealers."

Dr. Whyze responded wearily, "Yes, I know, but I'll rebuild my lab and continue my research. Then I will bring you evidence of the awful war on kids."

"I believe that," the chief replied, "and I will certainly contact you about any changes. By the way, is it all right if I bring Tommy a T-shirt I had made for him?"

"Sure, that's fine. We'll be here."

As the chief drove from the station to Tommy's house, he thought about his own six children. He had wondered and worried if they would try drugs, and knew if they did, they could become like the vandals he had incarcerated. He hoped they remembered what he had taught them. Kids in stable families are no different from those in the 'hood. Drug abuse doesn't care who you are. It hides in the shadows and around corners, waiting for you. Addiction is patient, willing to wait indefinitely.

Earlier in the day, the chief had stopped by a custom T-shirt shop and ordered special shirts for Tommy, Mark, and his own six kids, as well as a XXL shirt for himself. Tommy and Dr. Whyze greeted Chief Skeptical when he arrived at their door with a Specialty Tees bag in his hand. As the chief sat down, he apologized again for having to release the drug dealers.

"I know you both saw something and I know you are not liars. However, at this point, we have done all we can."

Turning his attention to Tommy, Chief Skeptical said, "I hope my own children will learn what you have learned and will speak about it just as freely. I want them to be strong like you." Then he unbuttoned his jacket to reveal the shirt he was wearing. Big capital letters read, “Not me! It’s a Trap.” Smaller letters below read, “I will not be tricked. I will not be trapped. I will not be an addict.”

Tommy’s face beamed proudly as Chief Skeptical pulled a shirt from the bag and held it up for Tommy to see. It read the same except it was signed at the bottom, “Thanks, Police Chief Skeptical.”

Tommy took it from him and said, “Whoa! This is so cool. Thank you, Chief.”

Dr. Whyze smiled as he watched his son enjoy the moment. He knew now that the chief believed some of their story and really was doing all he could.

“I had shirts made for Mark and my own six kids, but yours, Tommy, is the only one signed by me. I hope my children will wear them. That’s not all, Tommy. I have a plaque for you.”

He placed the plaque in the little boy’s hands. Tommy received it with a sense of pride he had never felt before. He looked at it and smiled but did not comment. His father looked at him with great admiration, confident that his young son would grow up to be a good man. As the chief was leaving, Dr. Whyze shook his hand and expressed his appreciation.

# THE RIGHT DECISION WINS THE BATTLE

## Halfweed and the Nopers Go to Tommy's House

The journey to Tommy's house was dangerous. Cars darted back and forth in the dark, predawn city streets. Halfweed and the Nopers never complained. They were determined to help kids recognize the trap and end the brutal scheme of the drug terrorists. Halfweed wondered if the scrawny, freckle-faced little boy held the key to their communication with humans.

Exhausted from the difficult trip, they finally arrived at the doctor's lab. Surprise registered on their faces when they saw the destruction. Halfweed cautioned her followers to watch constantly for drug terrorists. They scattered and searched the lab to ensure against an ambush. Halfweed saw the threatening message on the wall and read it aloud. "We will take you out."

"This is the work of the drug dealers that Hack sent to destroy Tommy's family. I hope we aren't too late."

From the lab, Halfweed and the Nopers moved rapidly up the sidewalk to Tommy's house, looking in every direction for their enemies. They searched through and around the scattered debris for Tommy and his father. Finally, they found Tommy in the master bedroom, and he looked unharmed. They recognized him from the picture at the conference. Relief flooded through Halfweed when she saw that Tommy was safe. They were not too late.

Tommy was practicing his presentation for a class assignment. He looked into the mirror and read his report aloud. Lethargic sat on his shoulder and said in his ear, "You'll make mistakes and the class will laugh at you."

Tommy sighed because he did make mistakes. "They'll all laugh at me."

As Tommy continued reading aloud, Lethargic said, "Your report is not very good. You will look like a fool and the students will make fun of you." Little Tommy's shoulders slumped, and his face fell. He felt self-conscious and read more slowly until he reached the end of his report.

"The report is stupid," he heard in his ear.

Tommy continued to practice, but now he was making more mistakes than ever. In frustration, he threw his papers on the dresser and went to bed. As he fluffed his pillow and lay down in bed, Lethargic whispered, into his ear, "You're not smart like the other kids.

They will laugh at you because you're dumb."

The Nopers heard every word Lethargic spoke to the eleven-year-old. Tommy tossed and turned, and each time he rolled over, Lethargic repeated critical remarks to him. "You're going to be laughed at. You will get a bad grade. You're weird like your dad."

Discouraging statements invaded his brain until he finally dozed off to sleep, hating himself. Lethargic moved to the table beside the bed, leaned against the base of the lamp, and went to sleep too.

# Halfweed Knows How to Combat the Enemy

Halfweed was thrilled. She danced and jumped for joy, and her followers couldn't understand why. Finally, exhausted and dizzy from twirling with all her might, she stumbled and her team steadied her.

"What is it? Why are you so happy?" they asked curiously.

"I know the answer. I know how to stop the drug terrorists—how to put them out of business. It's the kids! The kids can stop them. If enough kids refuse to use drugs, the terrorists might give up and go back to the sewer. With Hack securely locked away forever, the terrorists won't have a leader. All they did was follow the crowd that followed Hack's orders. They never thought for themselves. Without their leader, they won't know what to do.

"The kids need to learn that drugs always damage their lives. They need to know they are smart enough to stay away from illegal drugs. They are strong enough to stand alone and not follow the crowd. We need to tell the kids how unique and special they are! Each one of them is an original and there is no one else like them."

"How can we teach them?" Curiosity asked.

"We won't teach them," Halfweed answered, "Tommy will. He knows the truth because he saw the drug terrorists plan the war on kids."

The Nopers were uncertain if Halfweed's plan would work, but she had proven herself as a qualified leader. They wouldn't hesitate to follow her instructions.

# The Nopers Capture Lethargic

From the top of the lamp, three Nopers waited until they were sure Lethargic was sound asleep. They climbed silently down the lamp, grabbed him, and stood him up. Courage commanded, "Come with us."

They held tightly to Lethargic as he resisted and hollered, "What are you doing? Where are you taking me?" He hated being aroused out of a sound sleep after a hard day's work.

"Be quiet!" Courage spoke firmly in Lethargic's face. They dragged him close to Halfweed.

"You're Halfweed, the traitor," the prisoner snarled.

Halfweed said nothing, staring at him with something that seemed like pity.

"Why didn't you follow Hack and the rest of us?" Lethargic asked. "All the terrorists think you are weak because you didn't go along with the plan and follow the crowd."

She looked at her followers who still held the protesting terrorist and said, "Let him go and move away from him." As they released Lethargic, she motioned for them to stand back. Then she said to Lethargic, "The drug terrorists are wrong. It is weak when you follow a crowd that is doing the wrong thing."

"Hack will have you destroyed when he finds you, Halfweed," he warned. The Nopers broke out in laughter and Lethargic's face turned white with fear and confusion.

"What are you laughing at?" he shouted in anger.

They told him, "Hack and all the drug leaders have been sealed inside the executive meeting room. There is no way for them to escape! The rats have stopped using your drugs and are guarding the new prison. Hack will never get out!  It's hopeless."

"We will get more drugs for the rats," Lethargic boasted, "then they will serve us again and help Hack escape!"

Halfweed responded, "The crack rats are smarter than you. In fact, they are smarter than some humans. Even rats can see that drugs are a trap and they want out of the drug life. They've stopped smoking and using drugs. They are warning every new rat that comes to the sewer to stay away from drug terrorists. You won't be meeting in the sewer any more because the rats are taking over. Drugs have made you a loser, a zero. You go tell your evil friends that I have a plan to stop them and destroy their power over little kids' minds."

"You can't stop us. Nobody can! We've been around for generations. There are millions of us and only a few of you. Even if you destroy a lot of us, others will take our places."

With a stubborn glare at Lethargic, Halfweed said, "We are the Nopers, because we say no to dope and drug terrorism. You are a doper. Tell your lying friends we will destroy their power over kids. Tell them Hack is in prison and won't get out. Tommy will expose your lies and the war on kids. Go! Get out of my sight!" Lethargic turned and ran as fast as he could just in case Halfweed changed her mind.

"Watch me and listen very closely. The war on kids is the battle for their minds." Halfweed looked at her followers and tapped her own head. "If they believe a lie when they're young, they'll believe it as teenagers and maybe for the rest of their lives. That's why Hack's plan is to trick them when they're young, so he can trap them when they're older.

"Kids think they are missing something that others are enjoying. They believe drugs won't hurt them. Kids can't see the trap they're in, so they are convinced drugs are okay. Television, movies, musicians, and even some entertainers make it look glamorous. Liquor companies try to make it irresistible, desirable, and promote it to be normal. They run ads that make people think they need alcohol to have fun. Of course, they never mention how destructive the end can be. Listen very closely," instructed Halfweed. "The war on kids can be won by kids."

Courage protested, "Kids should not have to fight against drugs and alcohol! The adults are responsible for that."

"That's true, but many parents are too busy to help their kids feel unique and special. They think the school, government, church, or somebody else should do it. Besides, some parents are bad examples. We will do everything we can and hope that parents and caregivers will get the message. Kids are intelligent. When they understand the truth, they will stop believing the lies. We will start with Tommy. He saw how the terrorists were trained at the underground conference to trick, trap, and addict. The truth can empower kids to stay out of the traps."

Tommy awoke the next day not wanting to get out of bed. His father told him to get up, but he pulled the covers over his head.

"Come on, Tommy. Get up!"

"I'm sick, Dad," Tommy moaned. "I don't want to go to school."

His father pulled the covers back and felt Tommy's forehead. "You don't have a fever. What's wrong?"

He hunched over, holding his stomach, and said, "My stomach hurts."

Dr. Whyze took him by the hand and said, "Come on, let's have breakfast and talk about it."

With their cereal bowls in front of them, Tommy's dad asked again, "What's wrong, Son?"

"I have to give a report to the whole class today, and I know they'll laugh at me."

"What makes you think they'll laugh at you?"

"Because I'm stupid and I'll make mistakes."

"Now, who told you that?"

"Nobody," Tommy said, pouting. "I just know."

"Tommy, listen to me," Dr. Whyze said softly and gently. "Everyone makes mistakes. Mistakes don't mean you're stupid. It only means you may need to practice more. The truth is, you are unique and special. There is no one else like you. If you don't like who you are, and you try to be like other kids, then you won't become the wonderful person you were made to be. Instead, you would be a copy of someone else."

Tommy retorted, "I don't think I'm special, and I'm sure not wonderful!"

"Tommy, you're wrong about that. You were created to be one of a kind, to have a great future. If you don't believe that, you have believed a lie. Your brother has believed a lie. That is why he tries to be like other kids. He does not realize that he, too, is unique and special.

"The drug characters we saw and listened to in the lab were trying to get kids to believe lies. When you believe a lie about yourself, it makes you weak. Then you follow the crowd even if what they are doing is wrong. Knowing and doing what is right is the way to live. Anyone who says you are stupid is lying. You study hard, practice so you will be prepared, and do your very best. If they laugh, you will still know you did what was right. That's life—working hard and doing your very best. Now go to your room and practice until it's time to go to school."

Tommy returned to his room and repeated his speech in front of the mirror. Halfweed had climbed up to his shoulder. She said into his ear, "Tell the kids the truth about the drug terrorists."

Tommy paused and looked around to locate the voice. He saw nothing and continued his speech.

"Tommy, tell the kids they are unique and special, that each one is an original. Tell them they were not created to destroy their lives, but they can have a good future and a purpose. You can do it! Tell them there is a war going on for control of their minds. If they believe lies, their future success will be delayed and might be ruined. Tell them about the drug underworld, and convince them that drugs are a trap."

Tommy stared silently into the mirror and wondered where the thoughts were coming from. *Can they be coming from Halfweed?*

"Are you here, Halfweed?" Tommy said aloud. He felt his ears and his shoulders, almost knocking Halfweed to the floor. He looked around his room. He knew Halfweed was not visible without a microscope, but he still looked. He asked again, "Halfweed, are you here?" There was no answer. He walked to the kitchen where his father sat reading the newspaper.

"Dad, I need to talk to you."

"Sure, Son, what is it?"

"Well, see, I was practicing my report for school and I had a thought that I should tell my classmates about what we saw in the lab. It was as if I heard Halfweed urging me to tell the kids about the drug underworld, and that there is a plan to trap them with drugs.

But the voice I heard also sounded like me."

"Maybe you were having thoughts of your own, Tommy."

"I don't know, Dad. I'm not sure what to do. But I think I will tell the class what we saw."

Dr. Whyze warned his son again, "The kids may not believe it, and they might laugh at you. Are you prepared for that to happen?"

"Dad, you told me to do the right thing, even when others make fun of me."

Dr. Whyze felt proud. "As you grow older, there will be many times when you have questions in your mind about what is right or wrong. After you have thought it through, you will have to make a choice. If you feel it's the right thing to do, tell the class what you know."

"Thanks, Dad."

Tommy jumped from his chair, feeling relieved. He knew what he was supposed to do. Even though his classmates might laugh at him, he was not discouraged. He'd been laughed at before—so what! When he tried to play basketball, kids made fun of him because he was clumsy and not coordinated. Sure it hurt, but he had survived and this was much more important. Now that he knew he was unique and special, the hurtful remarks wouldn't stop him. He knew he could do his best. He put on his "NOT ME! IT'S A TRAP" T-shirt and put the plaque in his backpack.

In the car on the way to school, he asked, "Dad, what do you do when you believe a lie about yourself?"

"You have to replace it with the truth," he answered. "If you believe a lie for a long time, you will begin to think it's the truth. The lie traps you and has power over you. When you replace the lie with truth, you become free to be yourself."

"Thanks, Dad, see ya!" Tommy jumped from the car as they stopped in front of the school.

"Tommy," Dr. Whyze yelled out the window. "Don't forget how special you are!"

# Lethargic Reports that Halfweed Is Alive

Lethargic traveled to the school to report to Impulse. "Halfweed is not dead! She and her followers," he rolled his eyes, "captured me while I was sleeping. They are all alive."

"What?" gasped Impulse. "We saw her going into the big sewer. She was destroyed! I don't believe you."

"She's alive I tell you. She was at Tommy's house with the rest of her followers. And get this, they say we all choose to be either a Doper or a Noper. They call themselves the Nopers because they always say nope to dope and drug terrorism. Halfweed told me that Hack and our leaders are locked in a place where we can't get them and we will never see them again."

They were shocked into silence. Lethargic looked discouraged as he stifled a yawn.

"I don't believe it! Nobody could capture our leaders, least of all Halfweed."

"I believe it," Lethargic came back. "And listen to this. Halfweed says she will destroy our power over kids. Tommy is planning to tell about the war on kids and how we lie to them."

Impulse got riled up. "Are you crazy? Halfweed can't stop us even if she did survive the sewer. There's no way."

Hyper responded, "Nobody can stop us. We are the drug lords of the underworld." He pumped his arms, pretending to be powerful. "Kids are stupid and always will be."

"Spread the news about Halfweed and her Nopers. Tell terrorists from all over the city to meet me at the school entrance," Impulse ordered.

# A Battle Between Terrorists and Nopers

The Nopers rode to the school with Tommy. When he went inside, they stayed in the parking lot to discuss their plan. Halfweed instructed, “I will take Rebound with me to lead the way. The rest of you stay far enough behind so you won’t be seen. They will try to trap us, so stay alert. If someone gets caught, I will not leave you or forget you. I will work until you are freed.

“If something happens to me,” Halfweed looked at her followers and pointed, “Tenacity, I want you to become the leader. The rest of you listen and follow Tenacity as you have followed me. He will not stop until our goal is accomplished, no matter how difficult it becomes.”

When Halfweed walked into the building, she immediately sensed something was wrong.

Turning to Rebound, she warned, "Stay alert. Something is wrong, but I am not sure what."

Impulse stepped from behind a chair leg and threatened, "You are what is wrong!" Thousands of drug terrorists came out of hiding from behind furniture, doors, and equipment in the school hallway. They surrounded Halfweed and Rebound. Halfweed was startled. She had not anticipated this. She expected a problem with the terrorists in Tommy's classroom, but not this. These conniving thugs had come from all over the city.

Halfweed's followers were hiding behind the janitor's broom that leaned against the wall. They moved quickly, but carefully, to huddle as a group. They agreed to watch from a distance, hoping they would figure out how to get their leader and Rebound released. Halfweed would not leave them and they would not leave her.

Halfweed and her followers had grown strong as individuals. They had learned that standing for what is right is the way to live. Now, with their leader captured, they were uncertain what would happen to them. They were confident they had done the right thing by walking away from Hack and his drug terrorists. Becoming Nopers was the right choice.

Impulse looked at Halfweed with hatred, "I have been informed that Hack and our leaders are locked in a prison with no way to escape. I don't believe it. Lethargic said the little boy named Tommy will be used to expose our training conference and the war on kids." Thousands shouted, "WOK! WOK! WOK! War on Kids!"

Halfweed spoke up bravely, "You will be exposed for how evil you are. The truth will always overcome a lie."

Impulse's face contorted with rage. "We will destroy your little group."

"You may destroy us, but you cannot destroy the truth!" Halfweed fired back.

Rebound chimed in bravely, "The truth will always rise to the top."

"What is your name?" Impulse demanded from Rebound.

"Rebound," he responded with pride.

"Rebound. Humph! That's a dumb name. Why do they call you Rebound?"

"I was going the wrong direction, but I bounced back and now I'm going the right way. Why do they call you Impulse?" asked Rebound.

"Because I do things without thinking and I get humans to do things without thinking." His answer came so quickly, they realized he hadn't thought about it.

"Maybe you ought to think about that. If you do, you might rebound."

Without thinking, Impulse got right up in Halfweed's face and growled, "Even if Hack and our leaders are trapped, you still can't stop us."

"The truth will stop you," she repeated.

"Huh!" Impulse grunted. "You're crazy if you think that stupid little kid can stop us."

"Oh yes, he'll stop you all right. Boys and girls around the world will listen to him. There will be millions of Tommys—brave kids who refuse to believe your lies about drugs and about who they are."

"Halfweed, you're a dreamer. No one will listen to Tommy. We will trick him and his wimpy little friends into trying drugs. We'll trap them just like we have done for years."

Impulse was standing so close to Halfweed that their faces were nearly touching. "Where is the rest of your little goody group?" he demanded.

"I'll never tell," declared Halfweed. Impulse slapped her. Without hesitation, Rebound grabbed Impulse as terrorists grabbed Halfweed and Rebound.

Impulse raised his hand, signaling for everyone to stop. Then he put his fist next to Halfweed's mouth and said, "I asked you a question, and I demand an answer, now!"

Halfweed kept her cool and answered firmly, "I answered you."

His face red with rage, Impulse snatched Rebound from the tight grip of the terrorists. "Do you want to tell us where your friends are, Rebound? Or will we have to beat it out of you?"

Rebound didn't back down. "You can't beat it out of me. I don't know where they are."

Impulse told the terrorists to tie up both their captives. "We'll deal with them later, when we can take our time," he snarled. Pointing to one of the terrorists, he went on. "You head for the conference center and see if Hack has been captured."

The excited terrorists shouted in the background, "Come on, Impulse, let us take care of them now!"

"I said, later!" he shrieked. "Right now, I want them to see what I have planned for freckle-faced little Tommy. Go to the classroom! Take Halfweed and What's-Its-Name."

The angry drug troops were delighted to harass Halfweed and Rebound. They poked, slapped, and pushed them into the classroom where a large crowd of terrorists gathered on top of the bookcase.

Halfweed and Rebound listened as Impulse talked to the terrorists. "Now, go to work. Keep telling the kids how stupid, useless, and dumb they are. Convince them they will all be failures. Remind Tommy of every lie and bad thought he has had about himself. Tell him the students will make fun and laugh at him. We will bring him down!"

"Bring him down! Bring him down!" the terrorists echoed.

Impulse continued, "When Tommy arrives in the classroom to give his report, we will begin our attack." He signaled for Lethargic and the terrorists assigned to Michael and Chris to come forward. "Review the information on your assignment sheet. I have written some additional things that I want you to say when I give you the signal." He handed each one a small piece of paper. "Look at me and I will signal when you are to speak to Michael and Chris. They will repeat it to Tommy. All we have to do is sit back and enjoy the show."

From the Nopers' hiding place, Tenacity said, "Keep a close watch on Impulse. There will be an opportunity to stop them."

"What if Impulse orders them to kill Halfweed before we can stop them?" one asked.

"Impulse normally makes decisions based on his feelings at the moment." Tenacity was teaching them to understand their enemy. "He got his name because his normal reactions are quick, without thinking or considering the consequences. But trust me, he won't kill Halfweed. He will try to exchange Halfweed for Hack."

# I WILL NOT BE TRICKED!

## Tommy Takes a Stand

Tommy waited outside as students entered the school. A couple of kids from his class asked him about his shirt, "NOT ME! IT'S A TRAP." Tommy told them it was part of his report.

"Whatever," they mumbled and walked toward the classroom. Tommy was unaware that the war on kids had focused on him. His plans to expose the evil of drugs and the humans who promote them had made him the primary target of the drug world.

The small group of faithful Nopers was near panic after watching the capture and abuse of Halfweed and Rebound. Tenacity instructed them to be quiet and stay calm. He spoke with unshakable determination, "We will find a way, and we will get Halfweed and Rebound out of the hands of the enemy." His confident words calmed the group.

Tommy was the last one to enter the room when the bell rang. The terrorists with the special assignments marched down the bookcase while those who remained cheered them on.

Tommy would be the second student to give his report. He was confident, scared, and nervous all at the same time. Michael, a big boy who sat directly behind Tommy, was the class bully who had picked on Tommy in the past. He bullied most of the students with the exception of Chris, his bad-tempered friend. When they walked through the halls, they pushed kids aside, called them ugly names, and acted tough.

Terrorists rode on the shoulder of each bully, ready for action at any time. Impulse signaled the terrorist to whisper in Michael's ear, "That's a dumb-looking T-shirt Tommy has on."

Bully Michael leaned toward Tommy and said quietly to him, "Dumb- looking shirt, Tommy." He laughed at him, hoping to make him feel embarrassed. Michael felt powerful when he intimidated kids.

Bully Chris heard Michael and said, "Yeah, that's a dumb shirt. What's it mean?" Tommy ignored them both. He had seen other kids talk back to the bullies and get beat up on the playground or after school. Tommy had never had a fight and didn't want to have one now.

The bell signaled class was to come to order. Ms. Goodright, the teacher, instructed the students to be quiet. After roll call, she requested the first student to do her report. Obviously nervous, Sandra stood before her classmates and began to speak. Some of the students snickered and rolled their eyes in boredom. Tommy felt sorry for her and was angry at the students who laughed.

Impulse signaled to Lethargic. Delighted to do his job, Lethargic whispered in Tommy's ear, "Your mother doesn't love you or you would be living with her."

*Where did that come from?* Tommy wondered.

Prompted again by Impulse, Lethargic spoke to Tommy again, "Your parents got a divorce because of you."

Tommy often wondered if the divorce was his fault. The breakup of his family had left him feeling sad and lonely. Sometimes he wondered if he was the only eleven-year-old that had these feelings. *Where are these confusing thoughts coming from? And why now?*

The drug character continued with the discouraging remarks to Tommy. "The other students think you're weird. They think you're dumb and ugly." The negative thoughts flooding Tommy's mind were all things he had thought of himself. His shoulders slumped, and his eyes were no longer looking at Sandra giving her report. Tommy stared down at his desk. Before school he had determined to tell the class about the war on kids. Now he was terrified and dreaded the teacher calling his name. He sank lower in his chair and hoped the teacher would forget about him. When Sandra finished her report, Tommy realized he hadn't heard one word. He heard only the cruel laughter of other students.

"Tommy, it's time for your report," Ms. Goodright announced.

Frozen to his chair, Tommy did not move. He felt strange,

almost paralyzed. *What if I throw up, or faint?* he imagined. Other fearful "what-if" thoughts invaded his mind.

"Tommy," Ms. Goodright repeated, "come up here and give your report."

Tommy finally managed to get up and slowly move toward the front of the room. His bony legs felt weak and his shaky hand almost dropped his notes.

"My name is Tommy Whyze, and my dad is a research scientist. I want to tell you about a discovery that I made with my father in his lab." Tommy's voice trembled with fear, and his hands were sweaty. "One day I was looking at a cigarette through a microscope and realized the tobacco particles were moving around like they were alive."

Hyper, the drug terrorist assigned to Chris, got a signal to whisper in his ear. "Tommy's dad is weird. That's really stupid."

Chris blurted his thoughts out loud. "Your dad is a weirdo, and that is a totally stupid story. Dunce!" The class roared with laughter.

Ms. Goodright shushed the class, and Tommy went on with his story. "We could hear the tobacco particles talking to each other. They organized a conference to trick kids into trying tobacco, drugs, and alcohol. They plan to get kids addicted."

Again, Hyper whispered into Chris's ear, "Yeah, right, you little weirdo. You're just like your dad." Chris repeated the words in a whiney, mocking voice.

Before Ms. Goodright could correct Chris, the entire class was out of control, laughing and pointing at Tommy. Annoyed by their disruptive behavior, she singled out the troublemakers. "You boys will be quiet or I will send you to the principal's office!"

Tommy was so nervous that he wanted to run from the room. He stared at Michael, the loudest and biggest bully, and waited for the class to settle down. During the silence, Tommy's mind raced, wondering what to do. Then he heard a soothing voice. It was very faint, but he recognized it.

Halfweed's captors were so thoroughly enjoying what appeared to be Tommy's downfall that they ignored her. She had been able to move a short distance away from her captors so Tommy could hear her say exactly what his dad would tell him.

Halfweed yelled as loud as she could, "Do what is right. Even if they laugh at you, tell them the truth about drugs, Tommy." When Tommy paused and looked around at the classroom, he heard a different voice, the voice of Lethargic, who was sitting on his shoulder, "You little fool. If you speak the truth, they won't believe you. They will call you a liar."

The familiar soothing voice again said, "The negative things you've heard are the lies. You are unique and special. Tell them the truth. Tell them there is a war for their minds." Tommy smiled. He knew this was Halfweed's voice. He had no idea where she was, but he knew she was right.

"Please continue, Tommy," Ms. Goodright said. He looked at his paper and went on with his report.

Halfweed's interference angered Impulse, and he ordered the terrorists to shut her up. They dragged her and Rebound to the center of their group.

As Tommy boldly went on with his story, the kids paid attention to what he was saying. Though it was a lot to take in, they listened quietly. Realizing this, Impulse ordered his drug terrorists to attack Tommy's classmates. "This is a war for their minds. If we fail to convince them to try drugs, we'll lose this war.

"When Tommy tells the kids it's a trick, you tell them they will miss all the fun. When he says it's a trap, you tell them everybody is trying it. When he tells them they will get addicted, you tell them it's a lie. Others may get addicted, but not you. Now get out there and bombard them with lies—no fewer than ten terrorists per student! Speak loudly and clearly so they will ignore Tommy."

The terrorists never let up the whole time Tommy was speaking, but most of his classmates ignored the voices and listened to Tommy. Ms. Goodright got so caught up in his story that, for a moment, she nearly believed it. At the end, Tommy read what was on his T-shirt, pointing to each word for emphasis, "NOT ME! IT'S A TRAP" and in small letters, "You will not trick me. You will not trap me. You will not addict me." After a pause, he went on. "Police Chief Skeptical gave me this shirt and this plaque." He held up the plaque and read, "I'm a Noper not a Doper."

Tommy's final words totally exposed the underworld. "As I spoke, you each had a series of negative thoughts in your minds that were opposite to my warning. Am I right? You can believe my warning about drugs or you can believe the lies and fall into the trap."

When Tommy finished, the class applauded. Even Ms. Goodright applauded for him and said, "Tommy, you're a great storyteller. A young mind that can make up a story like that is an inspiration. The T-shirt and plaque were great to make your story seem real. One day you'll be writing books and making movies."

Immediately the terrorists whispered into the students' ears, "Your teacher doesn't believe Tommy's story."

Tommy hung on to his credibility when he looked up at his teacher and said, "Ms. Goodright, this is a true story. I didn't make it up. The police chief did give me the shirt and plaque."

"Tommy, stories like yours can seem real, even though they are only in your imagination."

He might have let it go at that, but Tommy was feeling empowered. He shook his little head and said, "No, Ma'am, this story is true. I didn't make it up. You can ask my dad."

Growing confused and annoyed by Tommy's persistence, Ms. Goodright looked at him and said harshly, "Yes, Tommy, I will call your father today after school."

When Tommy finished his report, Impulse signaled for his troop to return to the bookcase where he gave them their next instructions. "We must invade their minds. They'll soon forget what pesky little Tommy said. Lie to them like you've never lied before."

The dismissal bell rang, and kids hurried out of the room. Tommy walked with his head down, thinking, *I did what was right and got in trouble.* Just then, he was surprised to hear, "Hey, Tommy, I liked your story and want a shirt like that. Where can I get one?" John asked. Others asked too, and he felt encouraged as he answered, "Specialty Tees on Main Street."

Ms. Goodright stared at Tommy as he walked out of her class. Still confused by his insistence that his story was true, she walked down the hall to a seventh grade classroom. Pointing to a student sitting at her desk, Ms. Goodright said, "Melissa, may I see you a moment?" Melissa followed her into the hallway.

Ms. Goodright waited until no one could hear and said, "You are the police chief's daughter, and I want you to tell me the truth. One of my students told me your father gave him a T-shirt. Do you know anything about that?"

Melissa replied, "Yes, ma'am, I do. Last night my father gathered the whole family in the living room and told us a long story. Then he gave us T-shirts that say, 'NOT ME! IT'S A TRAP' Small letters say, 'You will not trick me, you will not trap me, you will not addict me.' He wanted me to wear my shirt to school, but I didn't."

"Thank you," the teacher said. "You can go back to your desk."

When the school day was over, Melissa recognized Tommy by his shirt as he walked down the hall. "Tommy! Hey, Tommy," she yelled. Tommy turned in surprise toward the voice. Melissa was waving at him.

"You're Tommy. My dad told me about you. He gave me a shirt just like that, only it's pink for girls."

"Your dad is the police chief?" Tommy asked.

"Yeah, he wanted me to wear my shirt to school. I will tomorrow. At first, I didn't believe your story, but maybe it's true. Why don't you wear yours again tomorrow?"

"I will, Melissa," Tommy assured her.

"Cool. See you tomorrow." His spirits higher, Tommy lifted

his head in pride as he left school. He turned slightly and saw Ms. Goodright stalk into her office. *She still looks angry. I guess she's going to call dad.* He thought of how confused and upset she might be when dad told her the same story. Tommy could not resist a big smile.

Ms. Goodright impatiently punched the numbers on the phone. After a few rings she heard a pleasant, "Hello."

"Dr. Whyze? This is Ms. Goodright. If you have a few minutes, I need to speak with you about your son, Tommy."

"Yes, Ma'am. I have time. Is Tommy OK?"

"Dr. Whyze, Tommy told a story in class today about drug particles that walk and talk. He said they planned a war on kids. I questioned him about making up the story, but he still insisted that it's true. I believe you need to talk to him about being honest."

Defensively, Dr. Whyze answered, "Tommy is a good boy, and I can tell you he does not lie."

"Are you telling me this is a true story?"

"Ms. Goodright, I know Tommy's story does not sound believable. You can believe it or not, but it's true."

With a sigh, Ms. Goodright ended the conversation, "Thank you for your time, Dr. Whyze. Good-bye." She hung up the phone and went straight to the school office, wondering how any of this could be true.

Dr. Whyze waited eagerly for his son to arrive home, and when he did, Tommy told his dad every detail he could remember. Dr.

Whyze responded, "You chose to do the right thing. You set the example for a whole classroom of kids. I know you will grow into a responsible young man who is a good example for many more kids and adults. I am very proud of you, Tommy."

# Impulse Makes New Plans

Over the next two days, Ms. Goodright and the principal, now aware of the situation, saw more and more kids wearing NOT ME! IT'S A TRAP T-shirts.

This made Impulse furious. He ranted, raved, and threw temper fits. He stomped around, cursing his terrorists and calling them failures. Then he ordered them to get Halfweed and Rebound and follow him. Impulse started down the bookcase and across the floor, staying close to the wall to avoid being stepped on like a bug. A squashed terrorist was of no use to the cause. They filed out of the classroom and down the hall to a seldom-used storage room. Thousands of terrorists delighted in poking and dragging Halfweed and Rebound as they traveled.

Tenacity and the team followed Impulse and spied on his activities, hoping to hear something to give them an advantage. As

Impulse and his followers headed down the hall, Tenacity advised his crew, "Find out what you can, and then meet me later under Ms. Goodright's desk."

The storage room Impulse had chosen was filled with brooms, mops, buckets, vacuum cleaners, rags, bottles, and cans of cleaning chemicals. He ordered his terrorists to sit down near the entrance and pay attention to what he had to say. "You will not go home with the kids tonight," he told his evil comrades. "We are going to find the rest of Halfweed's followers and destroy them. I'm sending you out in teams of four to search for them. By my count, there are eleven of them. Eleven Nopers and thousands of us. Should be easy enough, but I have to remind myself that I'm working with some world-class screw-ups!"

Impulse had placed spotters near the door of the storage room. He didn't know where the Nopers were, but he was certain they were nearby. His strategy worked. Tenacity and his troop couldn't make it down the hall without being seen, so they gathered under Ms. Goodright's desk as planned. They were safe for the moment, but couldn't see or hear what was going on in the storage closet.

Meanwhile, Impulse continued to instruct his evil army. "Put Halfweed and Rebound in separate corners of the room. Make sure they are each tied up too tight to move. Let's get some rest. When it gets dark, I will send the first team out."

As the afternoon wore on, the teachers completed assignments and lesson plans for the next school day and left their classrooms. Soon the building was empty and mostly dark, except for a few security lights.

Tenacity's team discussed options, then climbed with him up the side of the desk. To the tiny Nopers, it was as if they were climbing a huge mountain. Finally at the top, Tenacity pointed to a tape dispenser and instructed, "I want you to pull off pieces of tape. This will be hard work and you must not touch the sticky side of the tape, or you will never get loose." It took all eleven of them to do the difficult task. One by one, they pulled off tiny pieces of tape and dragged them to the floor.

Curiosity asked, "What are we doing?"

"We're setting a trap," Tenacity answered. "If drug terrorists can do it, so can we!"

Though they didn't understand Tenacity's plan, the teammates followed his orders. Soon they had formed the pieces of tape into an arch that looked like a tunnel. Once Tenacity approved what they had done, they dispersed to their individual posts to get some rest.

Courage had been able to make it down the dark hallway and station herself behind a damaged floor tile near the storage room door. Her job was to observe the area closely for any movement of the enemy.

Impulse's first team of four consisted of Paranoid, Schitzo, Repulsive, and Hyper. Their orders were to gather information. "Look in places where they could be hiding. If you see them, don't try to capture them yourself. Report to me immediately. I'll expect you back here in an hour."

The chosen four filed out from underneath the storage room door. Moving slowly, they looked everywhere for their enemies. Paranoid was jumpy, even scared of shadows. Schitzo kept asking questions. "What are we doing out here? Where are we going? Why?" Repulsive followed along, not really wanting to obey orders. Hyper couldn't be still. He was always moving, and when he got excited, he stuttered. "L-l-look for their trail. L-look f-for their t-t-trail."

Courage's hiding place allowed her to see and hear Impulse's team. She signaled with her hands to alert Tenacity of the four that were sneaking toward the classroom. Tenacity acknowledged her and cautiously waited for another signal. Surprisingly, no more drug soldiers came out of the storage room.

As a test, Tenacity walked to an open area where the enemy could easily see him, but he pretended not to know their location. The terrorists quickly hid behind a chair leg to avoid being seen and whispered to each other.

"We can capture that one and take him back to Impulse," Repulsive said, "then we will be super heroes."

Paranoid wasn't so sure. "I'm scared. We're supposed to locate them and tell Impulse where they are, not capture them."

"We can do this! I want to be a hero," Repulsive persisted.

"I don't see any signs of their trail," complained Schitzo, his eyes darting in all directions.

"Why don't we r-r-run back and ask Im-Im-Impulse what to do?" asked Hyper, bouncing side to side, barely able to stand still.

"Quit complaining and follow me!" Repulsive ordered. "I always wanted to be a leader. Now come on. Let's grab that traitor!"

All four of them ran from behind the chair leg. Tenacity ran as fast as he could, staying only a few steps ahead of his pursuers. His Nopers watched in horror, not sure what to do. Tenacity had signaled them to stay at their stations.

When Tenacity arrived at the tape tunnel, he hesitated. He knew his plan could fail if his pursuers saw the sticky tape, but it was a chance he had to take. He ran into the tunnel, knowing exactly how to avoid being stuck. Repulsive and the four terrorists skidded to a stop. He looked curiously at the tunnel and could see Tenacity had come out on the other side.

Eager to catch Tenacity, Hyper yelled, "He's g-g-getting away!" and that was all it took. Determined to be a hero, Repulsive darted into the tunnel and the others followed. Crash! Suddenly the terrorists felt a crushing weight on top of them as four of the Nopers jumped on top of the tunnel, trapping their enemy with a sticky blanket of tape.

The terrorists pulled and tugged with all their strength, but it was no use. The sticky tunnel would not let them go. They screamed in fear as they realized the Nopers had trapped them!

Tenacity signaled for the rest of the team to help him quickly roll the terrorists up in the tape like a giant rug. It worked! The Nopers struggled to drag their trapped enemies under the desk. They rushed back to their stations to watch for more terrorists to come out of the storage room.

While Impulse waited for Paranoid, Schitzo, Repulsive, and Hyper to return, he continued to make his evil plans. He summoned Meth, who was a cruel drug, and Tart, a crack-cocaine terrorist. He told them to put on their disguises. Meth was big and had long legs and looked very appealing dressed in the latest style clothes. His disguise included an expensive watch and a big diamond ring. He was Hollywood-handsome. Even the other terrorists whistled and yelled as he walked to the front of the group.

Impulse said, "Meth, you have been selected because you are so big and handsome. You know how to flirt, manipulate, and get the attention of females. I want you to use your charm on Halfweed. Get her to tell you how to find the rest of her followers."

"No problem, Impulse. She won't be able to resist me!" Meth said confidently as he swaggered toward Halfweed.

Tart changed from her terrorist garb to sparkly, stylish clothes. Her long, blonde hair and big eyes fringed with long black lashes made her appealing.

"Tart, come here," Impulse motioned with his finger. As she approached him, he smiled and said, "You were chosen because you can break the will of the strongest male. I want you to use your attractive appearance to get information from Rebound. Now go to work on him." Tart fluttered her long lashes and smiled at Impulse, who just for a moment wished he were Rebound. Tart headed to the opposite corner of the room to conquer Rebound.

She strutted slowly up to Rebound. "Hey, handsome," her soft voice cooed like a gentle dove. "Would you like to hang out with me?"

Rebound looked at her with suspicion, thinking, *What a dumb question, since I'm tied up.*

"I'm a little tied up here," Rebound answered sarcastically.

Tart continued her attempt at flattery, "All the girls think you are the coolest, Rebound, and they want to be with you. But I can help you get loose and we'll have a party." She squatted down on the floor beside him.

Rebound said, "Good! Untie me then."

"Well, you must do something for me," Tart said, as she blinked her long lashes at him.

"Oh, yeah, what's that?"

Tart moved closer to him, and whispered, "Tell me where your friends are and I will untie you."

"No deal!" he said emphatically. Tart moved even closer and touched his head. He quickly jerked away from her hand, wanting no part of her scheming ways.

"Rebound, I want you for my very own. I will treat you better than others. I'll be yours forever and go anywhere you want if you will only tell me where to find your friends."

She had underestimated the Noper's self-control. Rebound resisted every offer and finally said to her, "You are a cocaine terrorist. You deceive humans, and you are trying to deceive me. You have misused your beauty to hurt kids. Hurting humans is not something I am willing to do. You go tell your leader that I will never fall for your lies!"

Meanwhile, Meth strutted in front of Halfweed. He was a fine-looking specimen. He flashed his handsome smile and winked at her. Halfweed was wise, and before Meth could speak, she said, "What makes you think I would want you? You may look good on the outside, but I look for good qualities on the inside. Go back to your friends. I don't want to be seen with you."

Meth's smile changed to a frown. He slumped as he realized he'd been caught in the act. *How did she know that I am no good and ugly on the inside?*

When Meth and Tart returned to their group, Impulse announced to all the terrorists, "These two are useless and worthless!"

# Award Day Planned

"Hello? Is this Dr. Whyze?" asked the school principal.

"Yes, this is Dr. Whyze."

"This is Mr. Principal. I would like to talk to you about your son, Tommy."

"Sure, is something wrong?"

"No," Mr. Principal assured him. "Tommy is a fine boy and has never caused any problems. He has had a great impact on many of our students. Could you meet me at the school tomorrow morning at ten? I'll have Tommy join us."

"Sure," said Dr. Whyze. "I'll be there."

As soon as he hung up the phone, Dr. Whyze went straight to

Tommy's room and asked him to explain, but Tommy had no idea unless he was in trouble about his report.

The next morning, Tommy and Dr. Whyze met in the principal's office. They were both surprised to see Tommy's teacher and the police chief waiting for them with the principal.

"Welcome, Dr. Whyze," Mr. Principal greeted him with a big smile. "I appreciate you coming. Tommy told his classmates a remarkable story. From what I understand, you told the same story to Police Chief Skeptical. Is that correct?"

Dr. Whyze answered, "Yes, that is true."

Mr. Principal continued, "There have been questions about the credibility of this story, but it has had a profound positive impact on our school. Many of our students are wearing shirts like the one the chief gave Tommy. Some of our staff even bought 'Not Me' T-shirts."

Dr. Whyze and Tommy glanced at the principal's secretary sitting across the room with a big smile as she took notes. She stood up to display the logo on her shirt: "NOT ME! IT'S A TRAP."

Police Chief Skeptical said, "I have worked for years to warn kids that drugs are destructive, but Tommy has done something I could not do. He has helped his classmates and many older kids recognize the drug trap. They are making decisions to stay away from drugs."

Mr. Principal said, "The police chief and I want to give Tommy a special award to recognize his accomplishments. He's a hero!"

"That is very kind of you." Dr. Whyze was pleased and

proud. "Tommy is a fine boy, and I am proud of him."

Tommy was startled. The adult conversation swirled around in his head. He had thought he was in trouble, and now they were saying he was a hero. *I'm not a hero. I just did what was right. Other students wearing the T-shirts did what I did—made the right decision. If that's being a hero, then they are all heroes.*

The principal looked at Tommy, who was shyly staring at the floor. "What do you think, Tommy? You have done a great service, and we want to honor you. Do you want to say anything?"

His fingers locked together in his lap, Tommy never looked up. His legs swung back and forth because they were too short to reach the floor. The adults eagerly awaited his response.

After a long pause, Tommy spoke softly without looking up. "My dad told me to do what I thought was right. That's what I did. The police chief gave me the shirt and the plaque. That was his idea, not mine. Melissa asked me to wear the shirt again and I did. That was her idea, not mine. If I am a hero, every kid who chooses not to use drugs is a hero too." The adults looked on in stunned silence as the mature, unselfish eleven-year-old spoke.

The teacher who had questioned Tommy's honesty spoke up with excitement. "Every kid who will choose not to use drugs should receive a plaque, a shirt, a decal, or something to represent that choice. They are all heroes, but Tommy, you are the one who got it started."

"That sounds good to me. What do you think, Chief Skeptical?" Mr. Principal asked.

Chief Skeptical answered without hesitation. "Let's do it! Let's see that they all receive something for their good choices, for saying, 'Not me!' "

Mr. Principal turned to Ms. Goodright and said, "Prepare a letter to the parents about a special assembly, and make sure they all know they are welcome to attend. The parents can buy the shirts, but the school can provide plaques and decals."

"Give me the names of kids whose parents can't afford to buy shirts, and I will buy them," the chief added.

Mr. Principal asked Dr. Whyze and Tommy, "Is this OK with you?"

Both of them answered with a loud, "Yes, Sir!" As they shook hands and left the room, the secretary gave Tommy two thumbs up. He felt excited and nervous at the same time. His dad let him use his cell phone to call his mother as they drove away from the school. She was polite to Tommy, but there was no excitement in her voice. She did say she would try to come to the school assembly. As always, her reaction left him feeling sad.

# The Power Within You

Impulse was furious that every plan had failed. Tommy was causing a rebellion against drugs. Meth and Tart were unsuccessful in trying to get information from Halfweed and Rebound. The team of four he sent to find the Nopers had not returned. *Have they become Nopers themselves?* As he thoughtfully considered his plan, the terrorists he had sent to confirm the fate of Hack walked around the corner.

"Get over here!" Impulse shouted. "What did you find?"

"It's true, Impulse. The rats are guarding the meeting room and they've taken over the sewer, but that's not all. The crack rats look alert and healthy since they stopped using drugs. Even they don't want us! This is bad, Impulse, really bad."

As Impulse listened, he noticed a slight movement near the door. He couldn't see the Nopers on the other side, but he noticed a lumpy piece of tape under the door. The terrorists could hear mumbling voices coming from the tape. On Impulse's orders, several terrorists began to separate the pieces of tape. It soon became apparent that the tape was stuck to Paranoid, Schitzo, Repulsive, and Hyper. Impulse ordered them to pull, tug and pry, but despite their efforts the foursome remained in their sticky prison.

This situation seemed to overwhelm Impulse, who had maintained a fierce image. He lowered his head, shrugged his shoulders in defeat, and slumped into a corner to sit alone.

Tenacity gathered his small Noper team to discuss their plan. "When you know something is right, never give up. Never quit. Continue to work toward success. Now, with that in mind, we are going to the storage room to get Halfweed and Rebound." Shock registered on Nopers' faces.

Curiosity asked, "How are we going to do that?"

"The only power that drugs have is what we give them," Tenacity answered. "They have no power over kids unless the kids give it to them by putting drugs in their bodies." He motioned with his hand, "follow me," and walked toward the storage room with the ten frightened Nopers behind him. They were walking straight into the enemy's camp. Some of the Nopers wondered if Tenacity was brave or just plain crazy.

The drug terrorists were startled as Tenacity led his troops into the storage room. Impulse jumped from his isolated corner and marched toward them. "I see you have come to your senses and decided to give up," he barked at them.

"Not me! I've come to get Halfweed and Rebound. Get out of my way," he said confidently.

"You can't come in here and take over. We will destroy you!" Impulse blustered back.

The terrorists echoed threateningly, "We will destroy you and all the Nopers!" The four trapped in the tape continued to thrash about and scream for freedom, but no one could understand what they were saying.

Through it all, Tenacity didn't budge from his spot. "Stand back!" he said to Impulse, staring straight into his eyes and never breaking his gaze.

Impulse stomped his foot, waved a clenched fist, and shouted threats, but then without explanation, he stepped away from Tenacity. The Nopers stood with their mouths hanging open. Impulse had backed down. They heard him utter a few wimpy threats from a distance.

Other terrorists yelled, "We'll get him for you, Impulse!" They reached for Tenacity, but he put his hand up and demanded, "Don't touch me!" The drug terrorists froze in their tracks. The rest of the nervous Nopers were greatly encouraged by watching Tenacity take authority over Impulse and his terrorists. Somehow, they had not imagined that they could just say, "Don't touch me!" The words "Not me!" now seemed to carry a surprising power.

Though less confident than Tenacity, one by one, they looked at the terrorists and said, "Not me! Now, stand back!"

The terrorists continued to yell threats, but they all stepped back and made a path for the Nopers to walk through. Tenacity headed straight for Halfweed, while some of the others went toward the opposite corner where Rebound was tied.

Halfweed sprang up without any help, threw off the last of her restraints, and smiled. "Where have you been? What took you so long?" she asked.

Rebound looked at the opposite corner of the room and shouted, "Halfweed, how did you get loose?"

Halfweed smiled victoriously and said, "Stand up, Rebound.

You are only trapped because you didn't resist their threats." Rebound managed to get up on his feet and thrashed about a bit until the strings that held him fell to the floor.

With eyes and mouths open wide in amazement, Tenacity and the other Nopers faced Halfweed. Tenacity broke the silence. "Halfweed, you have known about this scheme from the beginning."

"True."

"Why didn't you tell us?"

"I wanted to see if you would give up under pressure or realize you had the power to make your own decisions. It takes courage to be a Noper." The entire team looked puzzled, and then they realized they were victorious. They had remained strong under the pressure.

Halfweed told her fellow Nopers, "I am very pleased with you." They gave each other high fives, danced around, and laughed louder than ever before. The terrorists watched in anger. After a few moments of celebration, Halfweed said, "Let's clean the trash out of this room."

Halfweed walked toward Impulse and said, "Go back to the sewer where you came from!"

Impulse retaliated, "I won't obey you!" But he backed away from her.

Halfweed was determined. "Like I said, go back to the sewer!" Impulse continued backing out the door while his terrorists followed him asking, "Why are you obeying Halfweed?"

Tenacity and the other Nopers joined in with renewed belief in their own abilities. Some of them pointed to the terrorists and repeated Halfweed's command, "Go back to the sewer!"

The terrorists continued their loud, empty threats. "We don't have to do what you say," they yelled, while stumbling backwards to the door.

One terrorist asked Impulse, "Why are we obeying them when we could be attacking them?"

Impulse hated to admit the truth. "We have to obey them because we have no power unless they give it to us. It's the same with kids—with all the human species. That's the reason we have to trick them. We can only control them when they believe our lies and put us in their bodies."

The confused terrorists asked, "Where are we going?"

Impulse said miserably, "I don't know. The rats have taken over the sewer. Is there any place lower than the sewer?" The terrorists began to run, dragging behind them the tape prison that still held their four partners in crime.

"Maybe to the city dump," said Spineless.

Halfweed and the Nopers forced the powerless terrorists down the hall and into a floor drain. They watched until the last terrorist entered the drain, still cursing and shouting threats. The Nopers stood defiantly until it was quiet. Halfweed broke the silence. "Let's get some rest. We have an awards ceremony to attend."

# Award Day

Students hurried to their classes. The hall was a mass of shirts—NOT ME! IT'S A TRAP. Every kid in Tommy's classroom had a shirt, including Michael. Chris was not at school that day. His parents were both drug users, and they would not let him attend. The police chief had purchased extra shirts to give to the students who wanted them.

At 10:00 a.m., the students went to the auditorium. Although attendance was not required, all grades were invited to see Tommy's class receive their awards. Only a few middle and high school students came to the ceremony. Dr. Whyze stood with parents and teachers who lined the walls. Some of them wore NOT ME! shirts.

The principal congratulated the kids for being smart enough to make mature decisions. He told them how proud he was of them. In unison, he led them in repeating the phrase, "Not me! You will not trick me, you will not trap me, you will not addict me!" It ended with a big shout. The kids stomped their feet, clapped, and whistled.

They were seated in alphabetical order with Tommy last. He kept a watchful eye toward the back of the room in case his mother came in. Each time he looked and she wasn't there, he felt a twinge of sadness. As each student's name was announced, he or she walked across the stage while the rest of the students and adults clapped. Mr. Principal shook hands with each child and gave each one a "I'm a Noper, Not a Doper" plaque they could hang on their wall. The police chief and teachers gave the students decals that said, NOT ME! IT'S A TRAP.

Halfweed, Tenacity, Courage, Cautious, and Curiosity perched atop a shelf with the rest of the Nopers and watched the awards ceremony. They clapped joyfully with proud smiles as each child crossed the stage. This was one war zone where drug terrorists had lost the battle.

"I will point out the kids I want you to go to," said Halfweed. "You need to tell them how unique they are. Speak loud and clear so they will understand."

Curiosity sat quietly, inquisitive as always. "Why don't we tell every kid?" asked Curiosity.

"A few kids have parents or caregivers who tell them they are special and unique, but sadly, many others never hear compliments," replied Halfweed. "Children need adults to encourage and praise them. We can't do the job of their parents, but I hope the kids will remember the positive things we have said to them. Words are so powerful. That's why we are the Nopers—because we know that sometimes 'nope' is a powerful word."

When Mr. Principal called Tommy's name, the students cheered,

"Hooray! Way to go, Tommy!" It made him smile in spite of his sadness over his mom's absence. He walked off the stage and up the aisle to his seat. It was then that he saw her at the back of the auditorium. Her face beamed with a proud smile. He could tell that she was totally focused on him. She did love him! Mark was there, too, standing next to her. They were both wearing NOT ME! shirts. Even his father, who always wore a suit and tie in public, opened his jacket to reveal his NOT ME! shirt. Tommy gave them a big wave and smiled so big he thought his face would break.

Halfweed motioned for her team to follow her toward the exit. They walked right out the door and down the sidewalk. The Nopers talked among themselves and wondered where they were going. Curiosity was trying to catch up with Halfweed to ask her, "Why don't we stay with Tommy and the kids?"

When all the students had received their awards, the principal announced a surprise. A popular kids' band emerged from behind the curtain and declared, "We have never been tricked by drugs, and we agree with Tommy. 'NOT ME! IT'S A TRAP.'" Then they sang their newest songs, "Not Me! It's a Trap" and "I'm a Noper, Not a Doper."

After the excitement calmed, Mr. Principal gave permission for the students to join their parents and meet members of the band. The Nopers were busy speaking complimentary things to the kids as they talked with their parents. Some smiled as they heard encouraging words. Others turned to see who was talking to them, though the words sounded like their own thoughts. When the assembly ended, all the students returned to their classes shouting out randomly, "I'm a Noper! You a Noper?"

Dr. Whyze noticed a puzzled look on Tommy's face when he picked him up after school. As they drove away, he asked, "Is something wrong, Son?"

"Well, I was just wondering what happened to Halfweed and her followers. What happened to Hack and the drug terrorists? Sometimes I think I can hear a voice telling me to do what's right, but other times I don't want to do what's right. Most of the time, it seems to be my own thoughts and there is an argument in my head."

"Son, as long as you live, you will have to decide between right and wrong. You will be influenced to do wrong things, and sometimes the wrong thing will look very attractive. You will have to decide within yourself what you should do."

# Epilogue

"Where are you going, Halfweed?" Tenacity asked. The rest of the Nopers listened carefully for her answer. They had all wondered the same thing.

"I'm going to more schools, and if you are a genuine Noper, you are going with me. There are thousands of Tommys in schools everywhere. They need to be encouraged to be brave and stand up for what is right. They need to be warned about the lies and tricks of drugs. We have to tell them how to stay out of that trap. So who's with me?"

"We are!" the group cheered. They were all busy slapping high-fives when Curiosity grabbed Halfweed's arm, stopping her in her tracks. A drug particle was running toward them. "Is that who I think it is?" Curiosity asked. "Maybe we should hide."

Halfweed, Courage, and Tenacity all said at the same time, "Not me!"

Shaking her head, Curiosity was embarrassed that she had so easily wanted to run and hide. “Yeah, I know. I have to be brave,” she said, grinning.

As he got closer, Impulse held up his hand and said, “Hey, Nopers! Wait for me!”

“It’s a trick, Halfweed. Don’t do it,” Tenacity warned.

Impulse was out of breath. “Don’t panic,” he huffed and puffed. “I’m not here to cause trouble. Halfweed, I’ve been thinking about what you said, and you’re right. I want to be a Noper.”

“How do I know you’re telling the truth, Impulse? How do I know this is not a trick?” Halfweed believed in second chances, but she didn’t foolishly trust someone too quickly who was guilty of trying to trick hundreds of innocent kids.

“Because, I’ve been thinking, which is something I’m not accustomed to. I’m not doing this on an impulse. Although that’s my name, I can change if I set my mind to do it. I know the terrorists will fight us, but I pledge to you and all the other Nopers, I will fight for what is right.”

Curiosity peppered Impulse with questions wanting to know how he got away from the terrorists. Courage patted him on the back with encouraging remarks, and Tenacity told him never to give up doing what is right.

“All right, Impulse. You can join the Nopers, but you have a lot to learn and must follow my instructions. Doing things impulsively will not be tolerated. Got it?” The Nopers continued their journey to the next school.

Meanwhile, deep underground, the drug leaders sat in their prison, watching Halfweed's video that had been thrown to them. Her strength was obvious as she spoke directly to the terrorists.

"Hack, you and your terrorists are totally evil. You take pleasure in destroying innocent lives. You operate in the sewer because you are sewage, real slime. Behind me, you see fellow Nopers who have joined with me to expose you. We will not rest until kids everywhere recognize that you are their enemy. We may die in our effort, but it is worth it to save the children. You will not stop us. When kids begin to mock and ignore you, you will know that it started with one strong Noper who told others the truth. Then they told someone else, who told another, and it will continue. YOU, and your slithering helpers, will be exposed for the evil terrorists you are!"

## About the Author

Charles Burton holds a Master of Arts in addictive disease counseling. His 35 years of counseling experience include his position as executive director of a 150-bed rehabilitation center and personal mentoring of recovering addicts and alcoholics. Burton's own struggle with alcoholism until age thirty supplied painful clarityof how addictions negatively affect families.

Burton is the cofounder of Overcomers Recovery Support, an addictions recovery program for adults. With his wife, Sharon, he authored the 90-day recovery workbook, *A Daily Choice, Overcoming Life-controlling Problems*, a personal study curriculum for adults in recovery. www.RecoverySupport.org

Years of front-line experience with alcoholics, addicts, and their families led Burton to the conclusion that the best way to combat addiction is to imprint children's minds with the dangers of addictive substances during their formative years. His new book *Not Me! It's a Trap,* is an exceptional presentation of colorful images and characters that will give young readers a clear advantage to respond appropriately when they are tempted to experiment with drugs.

"For too many Americans, this future is clouded by drug use and substance use disorders,which inhibit the ability of our citizens to remain healthy and safe and to achieve their full potential."
— President Barak Obama

"Drug abuse threatens everything, everything that is best about our country," he said. "It breaks the bond between parent and child. It turns productive citizens into addicts. It transforms schools into places of violence and chaos. It makes playgrounds into crime scenes. It supports gangs at home."
— President George Bush

Order copies of this book
and the accompanying instructor's guide at
www.notmeitsatrap.com

Volume discounts available for teachers, rehabilitation and juvenile facilities, and other organizations. The instructor's guide will assist parents, teachers, and group facilitators in discussing topics of drug use and encouraging positive character development.